Schaeffer Brown's Detective Observations: Santa Fe

৩ ৩ ৩

A MYSTERY NOVEL
by Candace Katz

To Joan —
for that next
beach trip!

Candy

THE BUNNY & THE CROCODILE PRESS
FOREST WOODS MEDIA PRODUCTIONS

First Edition. First Printing
Schaeffer Brown's Detective Observations: Santa Fe
Copyright © 2010 Candace Katz

Published by *The Bunny and the Crocodile Press*

Cover photo by Jonathan Katz
Book design by Janice Olson
Printed by Lightning Source

Library of Congress Control Number: 2010928382
International Standard Book Number: 9780938572534

For Donald Gibson, mentor and friend

With love and gratitude to

*Harold, Violet, Harry,
Wendy, Jonny, Cindy
and Grace*

CHAPTER 1

"It's never a good time to count your chickens."

—Will Thompson

Yᴇꜱ, I'ʟʟ ᴀᴅᴍɪᴛ I was down—but certainly not defeated! Didn't Chairman Mao like to say, "A journey of a thousand miles begins with a single misstep?" Something like that.

True, I was recuperating at home from the aftermath of my first solo case, recovering from a hairline fracture in my jaw, two now-patched-together front teeth and 15 stitches in my lower lip, but I was putting that behind me and moving on. I couldn't wait to get back to work at the Will Thompson Detective Agency. "To strive, to seek, to find, and not to yield" (as Tennyson wrote of the battle-scarred Ulysses) was my new mantra.

Rachel, my best friend and feminist lawyer, was impressed by my new-found vim. She had witnessed my descent into psychic immobility after a divorce and loss of job, followed by my new career as a private detective, and subsequently, my stronger and more determined personality.

"Schaeffer," she said, as we ate a nice beef stew I had made, eating in the breakfast nook of my 1940s little yellow cottage in North Arlington. "You do our sex proud. I haven't seen you this upbeat since our graduate school days. Do you think it's because you're once again unmarried and in a blessed single state?"

"No telling," I said. "Someday I'd like to give love another chance— and be able to eat solid food. My demands are minimal."

Rachel raised her glass of red wine in a toast. "Brava!" she said taking a large sip. "Just a few months ago, before you became a private investigator, you would have been lying in bed nursing your wounds, watching the home decorating channel and waiting to develop cellulite. But no. Now you're working out, learning Spanish and ready to get right back into the saddle at work."

Rachel was right. I was ready to climb back on my horse, and I was taking steps to get ready. What Rachel referred to loosely as "working out" was actually my new-found obsession with T'ai Chi, the Chinese meditative exercise and martial art. It's a meditative exercise when you do it slowly, but when you do it fast it's very Jet Li, and it's very well suited to a smallish person such as myself. The T'ai Chi masters claimed, in fact, to be able to fell five attackers at once with the ch'i (energy) from one well-placed fist. They claimed they could fight a two-ton force with four ounces. (Four ounces of what, I asked myself. Gunpowder?) But T'ai Chi turned out to be just what I needed to get my confidence back.

I found a teacher at a nearby strip mall named Zhang Li. Master Zhang, as we students called him, traced his teaching lineage, as T'ai Chi teachers do, back to the great Yang family of the Qing dynasty, and if that wasn't good enough, he had also studied with the famed fighting Shaolin Monks in China, who were the precursors of martial artists like Bruce Lee. Master Zhang was a compact, strong-looking man, aged about 106, whom you would definitely not want to meet in combat, mortal or otherwise. He was a taciturn but good teacher of the 37 postures, the punches, turns, and kicks. He was a quiet man, with a nasty laugh, which came out principally when he would line us students up in combat position and then push each of us over with one touch of his pinkie finger. He was not effusive in praise, but I practiced assiduously and once even got a nod of approval for my rendition of the posture Return to the Mountain and Embrace the Tiger. Like most of the positions with their elegant poetic titles, this one was meant to destroy an opponent's kidney at least.

৩৩৩

I was excited when I decided that I was strong and presentable enough to go back to work. I looked forward to seeing my co-workers again— Marna Wood, the acerbic yet grandmotherly blood expert, and of course, Michael Carr, with whom I shared a private electric circuit and someday, I hoped, more. I'd been in touch with them both, of course, but they refused to talk about work or to let me know how our new boss, Richard Don Thompson was. "Rich" had come from Iowa to take his brother Will's place as head of the agency.

So one Monday morning in early March, I got up at 6:30 a.m. to the aroma of a pre-set coffee maker brewing Colombia Supremo, a legacy of my high-bourgeois married life in McLean, and followed this invigorating smell down to my snug yellow kitchen. After a few gulps of the black life-giving brew, I pulled on my L.L. Bean rubber fur-lined boots (another legacy), guaranteed to keep feet warm down to 30 degrees below zero, and ventured out for the morning paper. The paper person (boy? girl?) engaged in a little daily challenge of hiding the paper where I was least likely to spot it, usually in the box hedge. This morning, I found *The Washington Post* behind the wheel of my aging black Jeep parked in the driveway. I picked it up and paused to do a T'ai Chi position of Stork sometimes called Golden Rooster, where you stand on one foot with the other knee raised—very calming—while you get ready to kick the bejesus out of an opponent. The sun was coming up, and it looked to be a beautiful bright March day, still winter but at least ambivalent about someday becoming spring.

Back in the kitchen, I poured more coffee, assembled the cornflakes and milk, and luxuriously laid out the morning paper. This was definitely a benefit of the single life. Every section of the paper was my own. I could check politics, local weather, the book review or the quintessential heart of the *Post*, the Style Section with its trivia and gossip. No need to share or negotiate. Didn't Thoreau point out how ridiculous and trivial newspapers were and how amazing it was that all over the world people woke up each morning with a desperate need to find out something—anything—about someone somewhere on the planet whom one didn't even know and whose joys or sorrows would be immediately forgotten? An apt observation, which like everyone else, I chose to ignore.

My need for news was satisfied this morning by dire prognostications on El Niño, more major nuclear secrets leaked (were there any left?), and omigosh, a story about someone I knew—Susan Gettleman, an old college acquaintance, who had won a MacArthur Genius award—an honor, I might add, that had so far eluded me. The prize was $500,000 for Susan's breakthrough study of the mating habits of fruit flies. Who even knew that fruit flies mated? I always thought that they sprang fully grown from bananas in a bowl. Susan had obviously stolen that award—with intelligence, creativity and perseverance. How annoying.

Still, "the readiness is all," I said, quoting *Hamlet* to myself, finishing my coffee and tossing the newspaper into the recycling basket. "Nothing ventured, nothing gained," I reminded myself as I pulled on my Washington work uniform of black sweater, black skirt, black jacket and black boots. At the last minute, I went back to put on a brightly-colored woven vest from my friend Rosa in Oaxaca, Mexico, for luck and then set forth to brave the cold in my heat-challenged old Jeep, which never warmed up till you got to your destination.

The roads were frozen and the untried Washington drivers were weaving gingerly though the sand-strewn tire tracks so as not to touch any wintery substances. As I drove the twenty minutes to the Will Thompson Detective Agency on Old Dominion Road, I did my T'ai Chi breathing and thought positive thoughts. I let myself imagine the gasps of delight at my long-awaited but impromptu return. Marna would smother me in a warm bear hug. Michael would use the occasion to embrace me just a little bit longer than necessary. My new boss, Will's brother Rich, would welcome me back to the fold, having heard of my prowess on my last case. People would probably send out for pizza and flowers to celebrate my reappearance.

Imagine my surprise, therefore, when I entered the front door of the office to find no one but a strange young girl/woman sitting at the front desk.

"May I help you?" she said in the manner of a saleswoman at United Colors of Benetton, conveying the suggestion that someone over 30 should be shopping elsewhere.

"Well…yes. I'm Schaeffer Brown. I work here. Usually," I finished lamely.

"Oh," said Ms. Brittney Wannabe, flicking a speck of imaginary dust off a snug black sweater, which barely covered a stretch of nakedness from nipple to navel. She touched a button on her intercom and said in a much friendlier voice, "Rich, a Chauffer Brown, is here to see you."

Rich apparently clicked off without replying, but quickly stuck his head out the door of his office. "Schaeffer," he said briskly, only his head and shoulders emerging. It was amazing how much he looked like our old boss Will. "Glad you're back. Meeting of all staff in my office at 10 o'clock this morning." And the upper part of his body disappeared again behind the closed door of his office.

No sooner had he left when I heard a sobbing-like sound coming from the back room.

"Is that…? Do you know what's going on in the staff office?" Goldilocks just looked blank. "Oh, never mind," I said impatiently and walked past the reception desk to the office that I shared with Michael and Marna. There was Marna, at her desk, usually serene and stoic, sobbing lustily into a soggy tissue, with Michael standing at her side trying to comfort her. Marna looked up when I came in but then just cried more loudly. Michael acknowledged my presence with a short "Hey, Schaeff," followed by a long sigh.

Well, so much for the flowers, confetti and long embraces to celebrate my return to work. Farewell to the luncheon, the toasts, and the general gaiety. I didn't know what was happening here, but it didn't look promising.

CHAPTER 2

"And though she be but little, yet she is fierce."

—of Hermia in A Midsummer Night's Dream

As IT TURNED OUT, my detective training was a real help to me: I was able to ascertain almost immediately that something was terribly wrong.

When the major sobbing had subsided, I brought a chair next to Marna, gave her a squeeze and a new supply of tissues.

"Okay," I said gently, "Will someone please tell me what's going on?"

"Well," Michael said after a short pause, pushing his auburn hair away from his forehead, "we didn't want to burden you while you were at home recuperating, but work's gone straight downhill since Rich took over. He's not a detective like Will was. He isn't even a real farmer though he does have that Iowan look. He's an agro-business man, as in take over all the family farms, have the government pay you not to plant and rake in the money."

"So what's he doing here?" I ventured.

"Oh, he's trying to shape up this place and make us into a Fortune 500 company or something. As he says, he's 'looking after the net net bottom line.'"

"He wants to turn Will Thompson's Detective Agency into a money machine," Marna said, "with no regard for human dignity or well-being of the clients or staff—well, most of the staff," she added acerbically.

"Would you be referring to young Lolita in the front office?" I asked. "I expected her to take out some heart-shaped sunglasses and a lollipop."

"Just wait till summer," Marna said, and blew her nose resolutely. Norma was a gray-haired matronly sort of about 60, who was good on stakeouts and just perfect for making enquiries under false pretenses. She was also the office expert on blood traces and compliance officer, who made sure that we worked by Commonwealth of Virginia regulations.

"Actually," Michael explained, "Rich's been taking out his rampant ageism on Marna. He keeps implying that she's no longer up to the job—which is absurd. As for me, Rich thinks I'm not macho enough because I don't carry a firearm at all times. He thinks we should all be perfect extras in his Dashiell Hammett movie."

Distressed as I was, I couldn't help noting how good Michael looked when he was angry. His hair flopped over his forehead faster than he could brush it away, his complexion heightened and his eyes turned a deeper green. I felt a familiar longing come over me in waves.

"But Marna, what do you think will happen to you?"

"I don't know. I may be too old to get another job. Rich says we're not bringing in enough clients. We should be advertising, chasing paddy wagons. I don't know. It's all 'the net net bottom line' with him. If I hear that phrase one more time, I may spit."

"Well," I said doubtfully, "I think you both do a wonderful job. What's wrong with this man anyway?"

"You'll get a first-hand look at the 10 o'clock meeting," Marna said, wiping her hands on her stained lab coat.

"Try to stay calm, Schaeffer," Michael warned. "Rich is tying to perfect the art of the put-down."

ꙮꙮꙮ

The 10 o'clock meeting went about as expected. The atmosphere was chilly; the conversation minimalist. First of all, Will Thomson's warm brown office, which we all loved, with its bookcases and comfortable chairs, had been gutted by his brother Rich. Instead, the walls had been painted black, and the only objects—the desk and the conference table, were black granite. The chairs were black and silver Bauhaus knockoffs, probably expensive and certainly uncomfortable. Needless to say, Will's signature picture of himself as a young boy, squinting against the winter sun and carrying a bucket of pig slop out in front of his Iowa farmhouse—where Rich must have grown up, too—had disappeared. In its place was a black and white abstract picture, the kind you order from a prints catalogue based on color and size.

Rich sat at the head of the expensive-looking black granite conference table next to the Britney Spears clone, who turned out to be a "Heidi." She was looking blank and chewing seductively on a blue Bic pen. Michael, Marna and I sat on the sides of the table and waited while Rich went through a few perfunctory pleasantries.

"Okay, "said Rich, taking a breath and launching into his agenda, "As always, we're here to discuss improving the net net bottom line."

I didn't dare look at Marna. I waited for sounds of expectoration.

"Schaeffer," said Rich, turning his attention to me, "For your information, I've made some changes here since Will's death and your absence. I'm trying to up the professionalism of the office and not coincidentally keep us in the black. In the first place, there's no more sliding scale for clients. Everybody pays rack rate. Second, Heidi is keeping track of your billing hours on a quarter-hour basis, and I want them submitted daily. Third, I want each of you to bring in a new client at least twice a month. Heidi will keep track of that, too. Finally, I want everyone here licensed to carry a firearm. Am I clear, Schaeffer?"

I was the only one not licensed.

"Well," Rich continued, looking directly at me, "I can't have pint-sized mini-gumshoes running around South America with cans of pepper spray."

That stung. I may be small, but I had risen to the occasion on my case in Mexico and had used the pepper spray to very good effect, thank you very much. I raised my upper body to its full height (5'2" when standing), like the caterpillar in *Alice in Wonderland*, and said with what I hoped was dignity, "Mexico happens to be in North America when I last checked, and my pepper spray disabled a murderer."

"Beginner's stupid luck," he muttered nastily. "The point is, we need professionalism here; we need procedure; we need profit," he concluded on an alliterative roll. "Who do I have for my staff? A dreamer, a so-called blood expert in her golden years and a Mighty Mousette who doesn't even carry a gun."

I was stunned into silence by Rich's epithets. Marna and Michael seemed resigned to it and Heidi was oblivious. Who knew a person could perfect this nasty repartee in Iowa of all places? Our old boss Will was as unlike his brother Rich as, in Hamlet's words, "Hyperion to a satyr."

Rich dismissed us shortly after that, and as I left Rich's office I considered giving him a quick T'ai Chi Golden Rooster followed by a very painful Fair Lady Works the Shuttles. Good judgment prevailed, however, and I followed Marna and Michael to our office where they caught me up on the case load. Nothing special. It's hard to be professional, pro-cedure-conscious and profitable when your jobs are hanging by a thread. I guessed I would have to get a gun license. I didn't really want to. When you mention "gun" in Act I, it's almost certain to go off in Act III.

CHAPTER 3

"As the Reverend Mother says, 'When the good Lord closes a door, He usually remembers to open a window...'"

—The Sound of Music (variation)

R<small>ING</small>. R<small>ING</small>. A few days later, I picked up the telephone and hoped it was news of an inheritance.

"Hi, Schaeffer."

"Hi," I said, cajoling a long-lost vocal memory to the surface.

"It's me. Elizabeth. E.J.!" she added for clarity.

Pause.

How could I have forgotten that voice? Elizabeth Jane ("E.J.") Lowell was an old college friend. Her words were followed by her signature throaty chuckle.

E.J. went on, "I was thinking about you the other day when I read about ol' Susan Gettleman getting the MacArthur Genius award for peeping in on the mating rituals of those fruit flies."

"Richly deserved," I said with similar enthusiasm. It was good to hear from Elizabeth and to pick up as if we were still in the same conversation. "Susan always made me feel like an idiot and that goes double now."

Elizabeth was a too close to be called an acquaintance, too distant to be called a real friend. We'd met and bonded the first day of the first week of freshman year. No one knew anyone yet, and we lived across the hall from one another. We were so thrilled to have someone to eat breakfast with that we kind of kept up this connection through college. We didn't have much in common except our proximity in the freshman dorm. Elizabeth was rich and aristocratic. She had gone to "Farmington" as she referred to Miss Porter's School for Girls in Connecticut. I could imagine her there, a strong mesomorph, with sturdy regular features and a shiny brown pageboy, in a white blouse and blue and green tartan skirt fastened with a large gold pin. I could picture her careening down the field hockey field, stick poised in mid-air. I could just see her sneaking cigarettes in the Ladies Room. Elizabeth was big-hearted and talked quickly with a well-bred raspy voice, only occasionally stopping to check her location in the conversation. She did everything with enthusiasm—with abandon. I admired the kind of security it took to take everything to the limit.

"Just so. Richly deserved," E.J. chortled. We observed a moment of silence in mock reverence. "If you ask me, you can never know too much about fruit flies." And she gave a great Elizabeth laugh, explosion, rasp, in one cacophonic burst. "But that's not why I called, of course."

"I didn't think so."

"Well, you put in the class alumnae bulletin that you'd become a private investigator—"

"Yes?"

"And I could really use a private investigator."

Ah, I thought, couldn't everyone use a private investigator—at least if it were safe, confidential and free? We could also probably all use a personal trainer, a Chinese chef, a professional closet organizer and a small chamber orchestra. I sighed inwardly at the thought of all those unmet needs.

"That's funny, Elizabeth, that you could use a private investigator, I mean—because I could really use a new client. Are you all right, though? Are you in trouble? In danger?"

Elizabeth laughed her raspy laugh. "Not in danger, I think. But, you know, I'm always in some sort of trouble."

It was true. In spite of her wealth and intelligence, E.J. had been known to get into very bad situations from time to time, which she dismissed as "scrapes," implying that they were the kind of trouble Tom Sawyer got into, say, with a concealed frog and ended up with a good whipping. Her worst scrape was in junior year when she went on a three-month alcoholic binge with some like blue-bloods from a Princeton eating club and had to drop out of school to go to a fancy detox treatment center. When I visited her there a few times, it was awful. E.J. had had the exuberance drugged out of her, and I wondered whether she'd ever get it back. Later, she became the principal of a girls' school in Manhattan, had a flashy New York marriage and divorce, and then I'd kind of lost touch.

"Where are you anyway?" I checked the 505 area code on my telephone call tracer and quickly looked it up on the online White Pages. Area Code 505 was New Mexico.

"I'm in Santa Fe, actually. I run a research center that my family trust, the Lowell Trust, operates. I've been here almost a year, and it was actually going well..."

I looked up the Lowell Research Center on the Web while E.J. talked—and sure enough, on the Old Santa Fe Trail Road, in Santa Fe, New Mexico, there it was, with Elizabeth Jane Lowell as executive director. It seemed to be a residential center where artists and scholars could live and work together in beautiful surroundings without the daily cares of normal folks. The center also contained a distinguished collection of Native American weavings, baskets and clay pots.

"Until...well," she lowered her voice, "odd things started happening with the rare Native American collections that my two maiden great-aunts, Miranda and Philomena Lowell accumulated. I really can't talk about it now. I need to talk to you in person. Can you fly out here right away?"

"Have you talked to the police? Or can't they afford to live in Santa Fe?"

"Very funny. I couldn't possibly talk to the police. It's not a police-type thing—yet. And anyway, my parents would find out and right now they think I'm finally doing a good job at something. My 'useless' anthropology degree is finally relevant. I'm suited to this position. I'm just horribly unlucky, I guess."

"Well, I can certainly come out if you can pay me."

"Payment is no object—as long as I'm in the good graces of Moms and Pater and the rest of the center's board. The Lowell Trust will send you out a big fat check FedEx, and—Schaeffer, I just had the most brilliant idea!"

"Uh-huh?" This did not bode well. E.J.'s enthusiasm was commendable to about the same degree that her judgment was deplorable.

"Instead of coming as a private investigator, you could come undercover! As a fellow of the center! That way, the Trust won't know I'm hiring a detective!" Brief pause. "Would you like to be a scholar or an artist?"

"Wait up, E.J. Slow down. Are you sure that we could make this look plausible?"

"Of course we could. I'll introduce you myself and cook the records, and—what'll it be? Scholar or artist?"

"Well, artist is easier." I couldn't believe how fast I was buying into this… "Scholars have to know things, but artists just have to keep their doors closed and look mysterious."

"Wonderful!"

"Could you send me a retainer of about $10,000, which would cover about two weeks, plus there will be expenses to be settled later. That would keep me on the good side of my new boss here." Rich's net net bottom line came quickly to mind. "I think I would like an 'away' assignment right now."

"Not a problem. I'll send the retainer to you, made out to you. It's Wednesday now, so could you be here by tomorrow morning?"

"Whoa there, E.J.," I said. "I need to pack. And establish a new identity."

"Tomorrow afternoon, then. You do some undercover thinking and call me to verify. I want you to meet me at the Inn at Loretto when you arrive. We can talk there without being overheard, and I'll lay out the situation in detail. We'll need to get you outfitted, too. Nobody wears little black suits and little black shoes in Santa Fe."

"But..."

"Trust me on this one," E.J. said with a laugh.

"Westward Ho, then." I said as I hung up the phone. What a great opportunity out of the blue! I would see E.J., earn money, solve an exotic case probably involving gold and jewels, visit beautiful Santa Fe, and not have to talk with my new boss! Now, I thought, all I needed was a new me.

CHAPTER 4

"Never wait for yourself."

—Surrealists Paul Eluard and Benjamin Peret

UNDERCOVER…UNDERCOVER. At first all I could think of was a trench coat and a wig. I decided to take a moment and do a few T'ai Chi postures to help clear my head. I practiced Golden Rooster, that one-footed stand, first on my right foot then on my left. I breathed in and out quietly and deeply, sinking my breath to just below my navel. I could feel the Yin of my right foot rooted to the ground and the Yang of energy emerging from the opposite hand. In fact, I was feeling pretty serene and refreshed until I heard an annoying giggle from the doorway and realized that I'd been observed in some pretty odd positions by little Miss Cuter-Than-Thou from the front office. There was a swish of blond ponytail as she disappeared from view.

Okay. I needed to be an artist. I couldn't draw (every human figure I attempted came out with enormous hands), or paint or sculpt anything more intricate than a piecrust. Performance art, chocolate smeared on body, etc., was out of the question. But wait. Hadn't I seen a kind of modern art for the artistically challenged made of cutouts, kinds of collages with found objects and decoupages? I seemed to remember an American artist who put all sorts of objects and cutouts in wooden boxes. I checked the Web for surrealists, bypassing Dali as too good a draftsman and finding—aha, an American artist, now safely dead, Joseph Cornell. Now I remembered those boxes filled with cutouts of pretty girls or wine glasses filled with blue marbles in front of maps of the night sky with the Zodiac constellations.

Yes, I could follow in those footsteps. I could cut and paste—perhaps not with that originality, design and creativity. And I wouldn't use just square wooden boxes. I would use all sorts of containers, like, for example, Chinese take-out boxes filled with sayings by Chairman Mao or lyrics from that awful musical *Flower Drum Song,* or both. The possibilities were endless, and the meanings could be subversive, evocative, profound or random, depending on the imagination of the viewer.

But did Joseph Cornell have any offspring? I flipped to a biographical essay on the Web site. Alas, Mr. Cornell lived a very private life in Flushing, New York, with his mother and siblings, surrounded by ever-growing stacks of clippings and obsessively collected objects such as thimbles, cigars and shoes. I read further. Oh dear. His use of boxes seemed to stem from his obsession with young women selling movie tickets in ticket booths. No. Not likely to have offspring. But…there were great nephews who gave his collections to the Smithsonian. If there were great-nephews, why not a long-lost great-niece?

At that moment, Schaeffer Cornell was born and needed to be raised, in haste, to full maturity.

"Michael," I called as he came in the door to the office. "I have a new client and a new identity!"

"Hey," Michael said with a smile. "You're two for two. I'm just my old self with the old clients, and we're getting mighty tired of each other."

I told him about going undercover as Schaeffer Cornell and he suggested that we make her a Web site, in case anyone wanted to check up on me in Santa Fe. For the next hour we sat side by side inventing the new artist using random texts, photos and clip art. We even put a photo of me scanned from my PI license onto the page. Of course, the artist's signature piece was a Chinese take-out box filled with unintelligible Chinese writing on little slips of fortune cookie papers.

"Michael, you're a genius," I concluded as he put a mauve artistic border around the home page and changed the Times New Roman font to a jazzier Matisse.

"You're the artistic genius," he said. "I'm just a computer hack."

I turned to him as we sat in front of the computer screen and gave him a full frontal smile. Gosh, I had missed being near him.

"Do you have any other talents?" I asked lightly.

Michael looked at me sadly. "I can make you a fake Virginia driver's license in the name of Schaeffer Cornell," he said. Then he reached over and took my right hand into both of his. "Oh, I know what you meant," he added slowly. "Talents like finding the exact right spot on your face to kiss first…" He put one hand through my hair and pulled me gently to him. I could feel his breath and caught a slight scent of a tweedy after-shave. His forehead touched mine as he looked down at our hands lightly resting together. He looked straight up at me, touched my bottom lip. "There, I think," and kissed me with the gentlest, saddest kiss I'd ever felt. He nuzzled my cheek with his and then kissed me again.

I closed my eyes and let myself feel his warmth. I remembered the night we spent almost together a few months ago in Puerto Escondido, Mexico. What was there between us? And what was keeping us apart?

Michael pulled back slowly, reluctantly, savoring even in withdrawal.

"What?" I asked gently.

"You know. I'm still with Anna. I'm committed, pinned and pledged to her. I just can't hurt her. She's given me so much. But I can't seem to be here with you without..."

"I know," I said a trifle wearily. I was torn between wanting him to kiss me again and feeling injured by his indecisiveness. "And she was there first. But Michael, when I get back from Santa Fe, can we just end this-this—whatever it is? If you're still with Anna, I don't want to be part of it any more."

Marna came into the office at this point, and she couldn't have been much of a detective if she didn't know what was going on between us.

"I'll take that fake ID, Michael," I said softly. "Let's talk when I get back."

CHAPTER 5

"Sagebrush is very fair fuel, but as a vegetable it is a distinguished failure."

—*Mark Twain*, Roughing It

W<small>HEN</small> I <small>GOT OFF THE PLANE</small> in Albuquerque, New Mexico, I knew right away that I was a long way from home. Inside the airport there were shops everywhere with Mexican and American Indian handiwork: blankets, Indian dolls, silver jewelry with turquoise, bright paper flowers from Mexico, even the cheapest trinkets, like the pencils with the slogan "more chilies than people" had a foreign feel. There were Native American drums and Mexican good-luck charms. Most notable were wooden statuettes of chickens, in bright yellow mostly, with straw sticking up as their tails. I found later that they came in many forms and were called "Navajo Chickens."

The food stands offered Tex-Mex in many permutations and strong coffee. There wasn't a Starbucks in the place, and that was only the beginning.

Picking up my bag, I walked outside to where the shuttles took passengers back and forth to Santa Fe about 100 miles to the north. I jumped in with two other women and the driver, a thirty-something friendly man, who informed the three of us right away that he wasn't really a shuttle driver, but a classical guitarist between gigs. Everyone in the Santa Fe area, I was soon to learn, was an artist of one kind or another, in spite of whatever he or she seemed to be doing when you met them. It was like being in New York and being served by actors impersonating waiters, only here everyone seemed a lot more mellow about it. Fortunately, when I was asked the inevitable question about what I was doing in Santa Fe, I could reply proudly that I was an artist about to take up residence at the Lowell Research Center.

The two other ladies and I introduced ourselves as we exited the airport and drove north from Albuquerque on Route 25. I sat next to a lovely

Asian woman, who, I learned, was going to Santa Fe to work as a makeup artist on a movie with Tommy Lee Jones.

"Tough job," I said, smiling at her. I meant that it would indeed be hard to cover up all of the craggy lines in Tommy Lee Jones' face *and* that it would sure be fun trying. On the make-up artist's right was a very pale woman of about forty, on the way to attend a conference about the newest wave in baby rearing: you carried the baby continuously day and night and fed him only cereal and brewers' yeast. I guess that made the baby lighter to carry. Yes, I thought to myself, Santa Fe is indeed a wondrous place, full of visionaries and artists and kooks. A perfect place for E.J. to get into a scrape.

Soon talk settled down and lapsed into silence as we began to study the landscape. The busy highway, which was once part of the Camino Real or Royal Road, as my tour book said, and which had in the 18th century connected the Spanish capitals of Mexico City and Santa Fe, was ordinary enough. It had its shopping plazas, gas stations and fast food stops. But the scenery beyond the highway, this late afternoon traveling north, was heartbreakingly barren and very beautiful. Being an Easterner, and used to grass, leafy trees, flowers, bushes and the like, I wasn't prepared for this austere landscape. There was no grass, just bare, brown dirt, for as far as you could see, till it reached the foothills of mauve-colored mountains. After taking in the brown dirt, I began to notice patches of vegetation, of which every bit was foreign to me. There were little clusters of rabbit brush, cactuses, and—our driver said—piñon trees, the piñons or pine nuts being a special Mexican and Indian delicacy. But it wasn't exactly the expanse of barrenness or the intermittent and strange vegetation that so awed me. I soon realized that it was the light. The sky was huge and the light had a kind of clarity, even as the sun was beginning to go down, that was the most beautiful thing I had ever seen.

Georgia O'Keefe had visited these parts, I remembered reading, and stayed because of how the light looked in different seasons at different times of day. It would not be hard to become addicted to the beauty of this sunlight.

As we reached the outskirts of Santa Fe, the woman attending the baby-rearing conference was dropped off at the Comfort Inn at the edge of town. Heading further into town, I saw that all of the buildings were made of adobe—sun-dried bricks made of mud and straw—which looked like yellowish, pinkish, brownish plaster with rounded edges. As twilight approached, the soft light brought out the beauty of the adobe color, creating shadows of blue and violet.

The lucky make-up artist was next to get off at the Santa Fe Inn, the only hotel in Santa Fe, the driver told me, wholly owned and run by Native Americans. I could hear haunting flute music emerging from the open doorways. The driver and I continued on North into the center of town till we stopped at 211 Santa Fe Trail Street in front of a remarkable many-storied adobe building, which looked as if it had been built into a cliff. This was where I was to meet E.J., the Inn at Loretto, a hotel made to look like the famous Indian Pueblo multi-storied cliff houses, a kind of pre-Columbian apartment building. The sun was just about setting now, and the adobe hotel turned a warm peach color with deep blue shadows. I was beginning to understand why artists came to Santa Fe and didn't ever leave.

This towering, beautiful, ersatz, adobe dwelling was to be my first introduction to Pueblo Native American culture that dominates this part of New Mexico. That is, its presence and spirit dominated; economic domination, I was to find out, was safely in the hands of the Anglo establishment—very rich white folks from Dallas or Los Angeles, who used their adobe mansions in Santa Fe as their off-season cottages. These Anglos were in cahoots with a small number of Spanish-descended aristocrats, who drew their genetic materials straight from Madrid and distained the majority of Mexican and mixed Mexican and Indian origin. A complex place, this Santa Fe.

As I got off the shuttle, several young men came forward to take my bags and usher me into the lobby of the Inn. It was a delightfully serene great room, with soothing water falling over rocks, a low-lighted roomy lounge with comfortable chairs set around a crackling fireplace, an ample bar in the back, where a gaucho-type was playing an acoustic guitar in a mournful manner.

I went right up to the hearth where I had agreed to meet E.J. And there she was, reclining on a stuffed chair with her feet on an ottoman, as if the years had not gone by at all. She jumped up and we hugged each other for a long moment. We both sought the comfort of the past, of the known, and where better than in our old school ties?

"You look wonderful," I ventured, when we let each other go. I had forgotten just for the moment that this wasn't really a social call.

"And you look completely wrong for this place!" E.J. replied with her hearty, raspy laugh.

"What?"

"We'll have to do a complete makeover before anyone sees you. Complete," she repeated for emphasis. "I can't believe you're still wearing the little black suits and little black shoes of a low-level Washington bureaucrat."

"I was a mid-level Washington bureaucrat, if you don't mind," I replied curtly, "and a black suit is always appropriate."

"Not in Santa Fe, it isn't. And particularly since you're impersonating an artist! In Santa Fe, there are kindergarten teachers—computer programmers—nuns, even—who look more like an artist than you do."

"Okay," I said, resigned, and ready for change. "I get it! Make me over. I'm in your hands....But tell me about the case, E.J. Why am I here? What's happening at the Lowell Research Center?"

"Let's talk while we buy," E.J. said authoritatively. "I want to get you to dinner at the center tonight. There's one of our after-dinner lectures. And I can introduce you around—to the 'suspects,'" she said with a wry smile. "Although it's hard to imagine anyone at the center who has the real-world skills to pull off anything illegal."

I followed E.J. down the corridor next to the lobby. It was lined with glass cases with showy but appealing Santa Fe clothing and jewelry. On one side, there were colorful Indian-inspired wool loose-fitting jackets, cowboy boots, belts, and silver and turquoise bracelets, necklaces and pins. On the other side of the corridor were the shops where you could purchase these items, but we walked right by them.

"You can't afford these stores, Schaeffer. Jackets for six hundred dollars, boots for eight hundred. Don't even ask about the trinkets."

E.J. marched me out to her car in the hotel parking lot—it was an old green Subaru wagon of some kind, clearly no longer made. Have you noticed how a lot of really rich people have jalopies for cars? Is it true nonchalance or reverse snobbery? We got in, jetted back out onto the highway out of town on which I'd just ridden in, and skidded to a stop at a suburban mall, which had all the requisite items.

I'm not really a good shopper. I go into a store with a list, planning to buy staples, milk, bread, dishwashing liquid, etc., and I come out with a variety of items that have no clear utility, let alone the possibility of being made into a meal. Recently I left a supermarket with a printout that thanked me for shopping, and a list of items as follows: wire garland shamrocks, painted eggs, mini-candles, and drinking straws with pink flamingos on them (six-pack). I decided to rely on E.J.

"This is just to get you started," she said. "You can add on authentic stuff later."

"The case, E.J., the case," I said, struggling into a pair of pointed cowboy boots for which I should have first braided my toes. "You told me that you are running a center for scholars and artists for the Lowell Family Trust. The center is built around a collection of Native American artifacts started by your maiden aunts, whose names I can't remember because my right foot is in too much pain."

"Those would be my Aunts Miranda and Philomena. Muffy and Fluffy everyone always called them. Yes, they were driving from New York with their menagerie of birds to Palm Springs, California, so that the birds, mostly canaries, I think, could winter more comfortably.—Yes, take the tan boots with the white stitching. They look great and you'll get used to them. So the aunts stopped off in Santa Fe to stock up on bird seed and loved it so much here that they never left. And we'll take that jacket in tan and orange."

"But it says 'Made in India' on the label," I protested.

"Never mind. Ethnic is ethnic and the colors go with our landscape." She swooped up a belt that matched my new boots, a woven scarf and a silver choker necklace with a pendant that looked like an upside down crab. "That's a squash blossom necklace," E.J. explained. "Very common symbol in these parts. Fertility, fecundity, rebirth, and all that."

As we drove back into town toward the research center, I got E.J. to tell me the details of why I was here: The center had most of its holdings in three climate-controlled vaults, but not all of its holdings had been sorted and catalogued. The uncatalogued items resided in one corner of a vault, which they called the "attic," to which only a few researchers and the center's fellows were allowed access.

A few months ago, the Director of Collections, Ned Gardner, unearthed in this attic a stunning artifact. It was a small ceramic bowl, which would seem to date to about A.D. 1300, the height of the ancient Pueblo peoples' civilization who inhabited Mesa Verde in Colorado and then Chaco Canyon in New Mexico, and then Paquimé in Mexico—leaving one great city after another and, for reasons unknown, continuing southward. The bowl was particularly interesting for its celestial markings: a moon, a star, and an exploding galaxy. There were similar markings on walls in the ruins of Chaco Canyon.

But even more than that, on the bottom of the bowl was scratched the words "Don Juan de Oñate," the name of the first conquistador to cross the Rio Grande from what is now Mexico to what is now Texas and New Mexico. On a brutal northward march, conquering Pueblo Indian settlements en route, and treating them in the most vicious manner, Oñate made it to Santa Fe, and declared it the capital of New Spain.

"So it's a pretty important ceramic bowl?" I ventured.

"Possibly unique. And valuable both to Native Americans for its special markings and to the historians of the Old Spain crowd, who trace their lineage back to pure Spanish blood."

"So it's a good thing to have found this artifact, right? Moms and Pater are proud of you?"

"Yes, they are. And we need to keep them that way. Unfortunately, we placed the bowl on a pedestal in one of the vaults inside a glass box, wired and triggered against any break-ins, of course. You can see it from all angles, even the bottom, with Oñate's purported signature."

"Okay."

"Then one day last week, our Native American docent, Dorothea Yahouti—who comes in from the nearby San Juan Pueblo three days a week—noticed that someone had tampered with the glass box. She told the Director of Collections Ned Gardner and me about it."

"Well, who was allowed into the vault?"

"Dorothea had led a tour just that week of twelve people from the Board of Regents of New Mexico Museums. But these are all distinguished folk. It would be tantamount to suspecting the curator of the New Mexico Folk Art Museum or the Palace of the Governors or others of that sort. Of course, many of the fellows at the center here might have access. We're pretty trusting among ourselves."

"Did you alert the police?"

"Of course not! First of all, the bowl is still there, and second, I might as well just limp home a failure right now. The Aged Parents are just waiting for me to mess up again. It's soothing to them in an odd sort of way when I remain true to type. 'There goes E.J. again; never could make a go of anything.'"

"I'm sure they don't think that way, E.J."

"Well, maybe not, but that's why I called you. I wanted to see if you could find out what's going on and who tampered with the display box, and see that it doesn't get really stolen outright."

"Okay. So tonight I meet a number of the suspects?"

"That's right. We're almost there. You go on stage in about three minutes."

E.J. turned the corner onto Canyon Road, lined with one fancy art gallery after another and sped around the curves with what I thought was unnecessary alacrity.

"Remember," E.J. said, "you are Schaeffer Cornell. You are a new artist-fellow. We were in college together."

"But I never graduated. That's why I wouldn't be in the yearbook. If anyone bothered to look me up."

"Believe me, Schaeffer, you're not that interesting. In this crowd, you're as notable as a random woman on the street."

"That could be my Indian name," I joked lamely.

But my words were drowned out—as we turned into the center's driveway—by the screaming sounds of police sirens.

CHAPTER 6

"Do we have roots? Are we real? Oh great inventor, we are sad. We must leave things unfinished; we must go away on earth: flower and song."

—Poem retold from Nahuatl

I'M SUPPOSED TO BE READY for these crime scenes, the sirens, the shouts of "keep back," the general frenzy of disaster, but I never am. Clearly something terrible had happened, way beyond the vague threats to the research center that E.J. had been telling me about. Maybe she had sensed that something even worse was about to happen. But as usual, I was unprepared to see and acknowledge the all too human toll in the world of detection. Human harm still shocked me just as it did before my "professional training."

Abandoned unceremoniously by E.J., I first lingered on the edge of the small crowd around the victim, now tethered to a stretcher. It was a thirtyish Native American young woman in native dress and long dark braids. E.J. rushed up to her and cried out "Dot," and I realized the victim must be the docent Dorothea Yahouti, who gave tours of the center's holdings from an Indian perspective and lived on a nearby Pueblo. In Elizabeth's universe, everyone had a nickname, presumably handed down at his or her prep school.

As I pushed my way in closer, I saw that Dorothea looked pale and still, her head bandaged around and around as she had clearly sustained a bad head injury. E.J. was holding her hand, and Dorothea opened her eyes briefly and seemed to recognize E.J. Then she gestured with her right hand toward her right foot. E.J. looked down to where the white sheet covered her and gasped when she saw that blood was seeping through. Impulsively picking up the sheet, E.J. cried out, clearly trying to suppress a major scream, when we saw that Dorothea's right ankle had been taped up, but that that thick red blood had oozed through the gauze bandage, leaving a wide scythe-shaped gash of red. With that, emergency medical technicians packed the stretcher into the ambulance and sped away.

E.J. looked pale and shaken, but she gathered her wits sufficiently to answer the questions of a nice-looking Hispanic policewoman, whose badge read Lisa Gabriel. She had the shiniest back hair I'd every seen, wrapped in a ponytail to fit through a hole in her police hat. On request, E.J. granted police access to the center and vouched for keeping her artists and scholars within shouting range if questioning were in order. E.J. asked if she could follow Dorothea to the hospital and talk when she got back and also managed a plea not to go to the press with the incident. Officer Gabriel granted both requests and entered the center.

E.J. then turned to two men who were standing nearby, trying to over-hear the conversation.

"Honestly," she said bitterly, "I'm gone for one pitiful afternoon and all this happens." The men looked chagrinned.

"This is Schaeffer Cornell," E.J. continued, "my old school friend, and new artist-in-residence. What a welcome for her." E.J. paused. "I'm so worried about Dorothea—will she be all right? I'm going right to the hospital to be with her, but will someone please tell me what happened?"

The taller of the two men began carefully clearing his throat.

"It's all right, Ned. You can talk in front of Schaeffer. We've known each other forever. She's seen me iron my hair. She knows Moms and Pater for heaven's sake. Please just tell me what happened."

The taller man was clearly the Ned Gardner, whom E.J. had talked of, the director of collections at the center to whom Dorothea had confided her fears that the Oñate vessel had been tampered with. I don't like to digress at a tense moment, but may I say, parenthetically, that Ned Gardner was the handsomest, most elegant man I had ever seen except for—Yes! Cary Grant. That's where I'd seen this look before. And oddly, there was something of the faded black and white film about Ned as well, before the advent of Tech-nicolor and Cinemascope had cheapened our most cherished icons.

"I'm terribly worried about Dorothea, too." Ned said quietly. "I found her outside the vaults less than a half hour ago, lying on the floor about when she should have been locking up for the day. It was awful. There was a huge bruise on the back of her head. I called her name and turned her over very carefully. She was unconscious. I called 911 and an ambulance came. I guess you know the rest."

"But Ned," E.J. said, "She didn't say anything to you? Do you know who attacked her?"

"No." said Ned regretfully. "The person must have come up from be-hind—and anyway Dot was unconscious. I haven't checked yet whether anything is missing from the vaults. The door was closed behind her. The key was next to her hand."

"Leave it to you, Ned, to omit the interesting part," said the second man in a rather loud voice. We all turned our attention to him, and he quickly introduced himself as Terry Franchot, director of programs at the center. Loathe as I am to interrupt the flow of the conversation a second time, I feel required to note that Terry was nearly as handsome as Ned, but in a completely different and contrasting way. While Ned's hair was gray-at-temples black, brushed off his forehead, Dan's hair was lighter, and boyishly short-cropped, his eyes bright blue, his nose short and straight, his teeth gleaming. And while Ned's limbs were elegantly loose in a faded gray tweed suit, Terry's blue, well-cut suit was filled full with his exuberant body, not at all plump, but at the ready to burst forth.

"I was getting to it…" Ned murmured.

"Not fast enough for my taste," Terry rebutted. "The wound at the ankle. It was a deep gash made with a knife. It was bleeding copiously and the knife was right by Dorothea's hand. Obviously this has significance for an anthropologist like myself, if not for a trader in artifacts like you," he ended with a sneer at Ned.

"But what does this mean?" E.J. asked hopelessly. "Who would have done this to Dot?"

A moment of silent consternation was interrupted as a third man rushed up and darted into our silent circle. "Schaeffer Cornell," E.J. said distractedly, "I'd like to introduce you to the Honorable Dr. Walter Scoggins."

The Honorable Dr. Walter Scoggins looked briefly at me with complete lack of interest or comprehension and spoke as if he were already in mid-conversation with E.J. "I suppose that my after-dinner talk is still on for tonight? I mean, I see no need to cancel, as I've prepared my talk and slides, although my notes are upstairs in my suite, and of course I'll need someone to accompany me—"

Dr. Scoggins showed no signs of abating, and E.J. was forced to cut him off. "Of course your speech is on for this evening, Walter. No reason at all to disrupt our planned activities. Wouldn't think of postponing your talk."

Dr. Walter Scoggins looked immensely relieved and actually wrung his hands. He was smallish with red hair, a red mustache and Van Dyke beard, and a nervous rodent-like manner, as though he knew he were at the bottom of the food chain. "So munch on, crunch on, take your nuncheon,"

I thought he might say, quoting the lead rat in Robert Browning's "Pied Piper of Hamlin." Actually, I was relieved that every male at the research center was not distractingly head-turning. I had no doubt that I would be able to study the good Dr. Scoggins with complete objectivity.

E.J. suddenly clapped her hands for attention and the assembled scholars, artists and staff who had come out to see what was happening fell silent. "Your attention, please," said E.J., with commendable authority in her voice. "As you are probably aware, Dorothea Yahouti was attacked outside of the main collections vault. The police are looking at the area now and Officer Gabriel will be by later to talk with me and probably several others of you." At that point Officer Gabriel came up to E.J. and whispered something in her ear.

"Please let me and Officer Gabriel know if you've seen or heard anything that will help the police find that horrible person who attacked Dot, and of course cooperate with the police fully should they ask to speak to you.

"I'm going to the hospital right now to speak with Dorothea if I can. Director Franchot will take my place at the head table tonight if I don't return by the start of dinner, which will be at 8 o'clock as usual in the Great Hall. Sherry will not be served beforehand in my office, however."

I happened to look up at Dr. Scoggins at that instant. He was staring at the ground and biting his lip in annoyance. Oh, no. The blessed sherry event would not precede his presentation at dinner.

"Of course," continued E.J., "I plan to be back in time to hear Dr. Scoggins's presentation on his current research into the myths and legends of extreme longevity. I know that we've all been looking forward to it."

Dr. Scoggins looked up with a gratified grimace, which by no stretch of the imagination could be called a smile.

I was just sorting out my own muddled thoughts—how wonderfully authoritative E.J. had become; how handsome Ned Gardner, Director of Collections was in his faded, elegant way, and how handsome Terry Franchot, Director of Programs, was too, in his own high-octane mode; how strange the gash on Dorothea's ankle was; how probable it was that something valuable had been taken from the vault—when E.J. pulled me unceremoniously toward her green Subaru.

"You're coming to the hospital with me," she said. "Officer Gabriel just told me that Dorothea's lost consciousness and that the famed Oñate vessel from the vault is missing."

CHAPTER 7

"It was not a pleasant business, Watson."

—Sherlock Holmes

OUR VISIT TO THE SANTA FE PRESBYTERIAN HOSPITAL was both useless *and* depressing. Alone in a double room, Dot Yahouti showed no signs of consciousness, but at least she looked peaceful, all tucked up in starchy white sheets that brought out the deep brown of her hair and light brown of her skin. E.J. sat on the bed and held her hand for a long while and talked with her quietly and reassuringly.

When we left Dorothea's room for a cup of machine-deadened coffee, we were greeted by Officer Gabriel, her cap off and her notebook out. As I'd already noticed, Officer Gabriel was professional and efficient, if a trifle burned out.

Methodically, she went through a series of questions with E.J.: she verified that Dorothea lived about 45 minutes away at San Juan Pueblo, one of the several Native American sovereign nations, what I would have called "reservations," within the state of New Mexico that grew up along the Rio Grande river north of Albuquerque to Santa Fe and ending in Taos Pueblo in the mountains and branching out west of Albuquerque towards Gallup, New Mexico. Like the others, San Juan Pueblo was self-governing with its own governor and police force. San Juan Pueblo was Tewa-speaking, with Spanish as a second language.

Officer G. recorded that Dorothea had been employed as a Native American docent for more than a year in a program that E.J. and Ned had started to give contemporary native interpretation to the rare Indian objects on display in the vaults, which had largely been valued and studied for their aesthetics, antiquity and rarity without acknowledgement of their religious, ritualistic or practical significance, which seemed not to have changed much over time. The new program, E.J. continued, included bringing in student docents from different Pueblos several times a week to help out with the school groups.

Probably noticing that the list of suspects had just enlarged exponentially both in number and geographically to around the state, Officer Gabriel lapsed into passionate mutterings to herself in very fast Spanish. It could have been a grocery list, a list of curses, or a series of Hail Marys, I couldn't be sure.

When the muttering stopped, E.J. explained that she was first alerted to a problem several days ago when Dorothea reported to her and Ned that the protective glass surrounding their most prized item, the Oñate vessel, seemed to have been tampered with.

"Did you find it strange that Dorothea went to Ned as well as you?" Office G. queried.

"Not really," E.J. shrugged. "Ned is in charge of collections. He's a great expert on weavings, pottery, baskets and other artifacts, dolls, headdresses, ceremonial jewelry—all the artifacts in our collections, some of them dating back over a thousand years. And it was Ned who found the Oñate vessel in the first place—in our undocumented 'attic' room. All of the artifacts in Ned's charge are kept in state of the art conditions in our vaults to protect them for future generations."

"What did Dorothea mean by the glass being tampered with?" the officer asked sharply.

"Well, it was partly a feeling, she said, and partly a sense that the glass cover had been put back in a slightly different way into its grooves than the way she had seen it before. Did you find any fingerprints?'

"We've lifted prints, of course, but there's no reason that there shouldn't be a print for every fellow in the center, as well as every visitor, plus the board of directors, plus the Mormon Tabernacle Choir, for all I know." Officer Gabriel started sputtering in Spanish again. Gathering herself back together and running her hands through her long ponytail in a practiced gesture, Officer Gabriel continued: "Do you know if Dorothea had any enemies? Could this be something other than a robbery interrupted? Do you know why Ms. Yahouti's ankle was slashed?"

I really liked Officer Gabriel. Not only did she look great in her khaki uniform with her long dark hair, but she was asking all the things I wanted to know.

"I'm sure that Dot had no enemies," E.J. replied stoutly. "Everyone loved her. She was gracious and really loved her job. About the ankle—

maybe someone didn't want her to walk away?"

Officer Gabriel let out a few more curse words in Spanish. I had no idea what she was saying but it didn't sound polite. As you may know, my high school conversational Spanish language skills have proved completely inadequate to any of my on-the-spot professional needs, even though I believe I could translate a little *Don Quixote* if push came to shove. Surprisingly enough, this ability has not yet come in handy.

"Officer Gabriel," Dot said. "I have a favor to ask. You know that I run this center as part of my family foundation. I'd be really grateful if could keep this matter quiet while you're investigating."

Officer Gabriel sighed and closed her notebook. "All right. But I can't vouch for anyone else." She paused. "I'll need to put a guard on Dorothea's door. Can you cover the cost of a security guard?"

"Of course. I should have thought of that. Is Dot still in danger?"

"I'd say so. She saw something she shouldn't have or did something she shouldn't have, and someone is angry. Let's hope this is a warning only. Because if there's more melodrama here, there's no way you're going to keep your precious research center from sharing the front page of *People* magazine with Angelina Jolie."

E.J. was chastened. "Yes, Officer Gabriel."

"I have a favor to ask you, Ms. Lowell. I tried to reach Dorothea Yahouti's next of kin, who comes up in my records as husband Simon Yahouti, no current address, but a P.O. Box number in Gallup. Do you know him?"

"I've never met him, but I knew that Dot is married to a part Hopi, part Acoma Pueblo Indian. I think he lives west of Albuquerque, maybe on Hopi land out there or maybe in Acoma Pueblo. Dot mostly lives here at San Juan Pueblo, for her job. And her family's here."

"Okay. If I stay here and work this end, could you go out to San Juan Pueblo tomorrow and break the news to her family? And try to reach her husband Simon?"

"Of course," said E.J. "Glad that I have my old pal Schaeffer here to help me out." She gave my arm a squeeze. I was surprised at how much trouble it seemed to take to dampen E.J.'s can-do spirit. I guess that's why she was always in trouble.

All three of us drove back to the research center and slipped into the back of the great hall in time for the peroration of the Honorable Dr. Walter

J. Scoggins's anthropological talk on the "Legends of Longevity."

"On a humorous final note," he was just concluding, "I give you a taste of the omnipresent fascination with long life from"—here he fumbled lovingly with a tattered and yellowed newspaper article—"the *San Francisco Chronicle* of 1985. It describes a birthday party honoring a particular Australian lungfish, which you may know is an eel-like, scale-covered, forty-foot denizen of the sea, thought by many to be the missing link between fish and amphibians because it can live underwater and also breathe air. In that way it might be called a 'proto-amphibian' and, thus"—here Dr. Scoggins paused for effect for what can charitably be described as academic humor—"this lungfish could easily be one of the ancestors of those seated around the table today!" There was a short pause, but polite laughter failed to materialize. "In any case, our relative, the Australian lungfish was acquired by the San Francisco aquarium in 1928 as a fully-developed adult. He is, therefore, at least 65 years old and the oldest fish in captivity. Is it any wonder that he is called 'Methuselah' after the Old Testament's millennium-aged figure?" Dr. Scoggins straightened his papers and sat down.

"Could anyone have drawn that fish-story out any longer?" I whispered to E.J.

"Could anyone have made it less interesting?" she whispered back.

At the same moment, up popped Terry Franchot leading the somewhat dutiful applause with enthusiasm. "Thank you so much for that informative talk, Dr. Scoggins. I'm sure that all the fellows here appreciate your sharing your current research—and for making us all feel so young." Dr. Franchot chuckled with appreciation at his own remark. Terry had caught E.J.'s eye earlier when we had entered the back of the great hall, but Terry remained standing, reluctant to leave the limelight. Instead, he raised his glass in a traditional toast: "To Dr. Scoggins, and to the founders of the research center, Miranda and Philomena Lowell, for making all this possible."

E.J. turned to me and whispered," If I didn't know better, I'd swear he was after my job."

"He does have a certain snake-in-the-grass-like quality," I agreed. Like Cassius in *Julius Caesar*, Terry Franchot managed to have a "lean and hungry look"—in spite of being so obviously well-fed.

"Ahem," said E.J. loudly from the back of the room. "Thank you,

Dr. Franchot, for filling in for me on short notice and special thanks to Dr. Scoggins for his fascinating talk. We are very much in your debt." Dr. Scoggins bowed slightly and his red Van Dyke beard met his tasteful light blue tie. "I'd like to take this occasion to introduce an artist and good friend, Schaeffer Cornell, who will be joining us as an artist in residence at the center. Some of you may know her work in a variety of media." E.J. paused. "Finally, I am sorry to report that Dorothea Yahouti's condition is serious and unchanged. Officer Gabriel of the Santa Fe Police Force will be investigating this horrible crime, and I hope that you will be available for her should she have any questions for you. Should you wish to speak with her yourself, she will be in my office for the next hour or so."

Officer Gabriel, E.J., and I walked rapidly out the door of the great hall and into the adjoining building, which housed the center's offices and the vaults. As beautiful as the great dining hall was, in its simple Spanish colonial details, E.J.'s office was smaller but even more spectacular in its way. The indomitable and fabulously rich Lowell spinsters, Miranda and Philomena, had collected everything beautiful and intriguing that had come their way. After entering the office, we descended a carved wooden stairway into a large rectangular room, both warm and awe-inspiring at the same time. At the far end was a magnificent fireplace, with a crackling fire and topped not by a mantle piece but by what seemed to be a Renaissance Spanish altar piece in three parts, with the central panel a magnificent Virgin Mary in oils. Spanish majolica tiles in blue and white designs finished off the wall of the fireplace. Eight deep maroon leather chairs, with brass upholstery tacks were set around the fireplace with a solid wooden table in the middle. Grapes, soft cheeses, fresh bread, water, white wine, the local piñon nuts and olives had been set out on wooden platters, pitchers and blue and white ceramic bowls.

The ceiling of E.J.'s office was about twenty feet high, in a cross-timbered style, which I came to recognize as Spanish missionary style, the large cross timbers called vegas and the smaller lattice work called latillas. The walls were lined with bookcases, which held books and periodicals, and what looked to be ancient and irreplaceable Native American pots. E.J.'s large oaken desk had the usual scattering of papers, and, oddly, circling three sides of the desk, about a dozen realistic ceramic replicas of parakeets, more than four-times life size. I made a note to myself to ask E.J. about them.

Officer Gabriel, E.J. and I sat down in the leather chairs and helped ourselves to cheese, bread and grapes. I found myself unaccountably thirsty and downed three glasses of delicious, cold, crisp water in quick succession.

"I warned you about the altitude, didn't I?" E.J. said, as I filled my glass again. "Santa Fe is about 7,000 feet above sea level. Washington, D.C., is about a foot and a half above sea level—when it isn't raining. So keep drinking water and don't even think about having an alcoholic beverage before Friday." I nodded politely, secretly having planned to put myself to bed with a nice stiff drink. This had been an awfully long day, what with the traveling, the altitude, the time zone change adding two extra hours to my day, the rapid volley of clothes shopping, the attack on Dorothea, to say nothing about just being around E.J.

"And expect bad dreams for the next week or two. The altitude has a disturbing influence on your sleep patterns." So there was to be no rest for the weary. I guess that's why they call this "work."

Not surprisingly, the first to knock on the door was Terry Franchot, Director of Programs. Terry was energetic, I'll give him that, and handsome, I admitted reluctantly. He clearly thought of himself as a ladies' man, approaching each of us three women, one at a time, as if each was the only woman in the room, or for that matter, the universe. He embraced E.J., somewhat to her discomfort, and in a low voice offered any and all help in his power to ameliorate this disastrous situation. Next he held my hand, reintroducing himself, for at least a beat longer than necessary, and looked deeply into my eyes. His were a deep blue. He murmured that he was happy to know me and that he respected my work. For that one moment, I did feel his vitality and charm sweep over me. Immediately afterwards, remembering that I didn't have any work to admire, I wondered whether he was just an imaginative liar or he was already suspicious of my false cover and wanted to rattle me. In either case, the courtship was over.

Officer Gabriel got the Terry treatment last, but by no means least. He introduced himself as Dr. Franchot ("that's Fran-SHOW") and greeted her in, what to my ear, was flawless and idiomatic Spanish. He ended in English saying that he was a student of the peoples of this complex region for the last 20 years. It may have been my imagination, but Officer Gabriel's complexion seemed to heighten prettily, her amber eyes to glow, and her officer's cap to come unaccountably askew, at which point, as if it had suddenly gotten hot in the room, she took the cap off and let her shiny black hair luxuriate to full advantage.

Terry Franchot than took a seat next to Officer Gabriel and turned expectantly to E.J., with a glance at me. Sensing his curiosity, E.J. explained that I was here as her old friend for moral support, and that since I had only arrived today, could have had nothing to do with tampering or the attack on Dorothea. The explanation had an odd, soothing effect on Terry. He was mentally judging me harmless, someone who didn't have to be reckoned with, and someone who would not stand between him and the throne. On the other hand, as E.J.'s close friend and confidante, I couldn't be totally ignored. But mostly registering relief, Terry went on a short rant.

"E.J., you know I've never liked the security at our vaults here at the center. Your aunts collected some of the finest artifacts from 1000 years ago—examples of all the major pottery, weaving and basketry styles of the great tribes of the Southwest, as well as other major artifacts such as Katsina dolls and jewelry. And your aunts left the money to care for them properly in climate-controlled, moisture-proof vaults so that they would be here for future generations of students and scholars." Terry was working himself up now and rather enjoying himself. "Oh, I know that this is Ned's bailiwick as Director of Collections. But could he be any more lax? Why do we still have keys and sign-out books like a 19th-century gentleman's library when we should have machines that recognize the iris of your eye or at very least the sound-waves of your voice? If it were my job..."

"Ned and I will certainly take your ideas into consideration, Terry," E.J. said diplomatically.

Officer Gabriel had stopped fidgeting with her hair by then and looked all business. "Dr. Franchot," she asked sternly, "can you shed any light on who may have taken the Oñate vessel or who has attacked Ms. Yahouti in such a brutal manner?"

"Well, as I say, with the lax security here, it could have been anyone. But I wouldn't discount Dorothea or her associates. Ned and E.J. both know that I have been completely opposed to allowing Native docents in the vaults, and that goes double for the young people from the Pueblos that Dorothea has brought in as interns. Only certified scholars or researchers should ever be allowed to enter the vaults, and then only with impeccable letters of introduction."

"Right," Officer Gabriel said, "and what would be Ms. Yahouti's motive? For having herself attacked, for example?"

"Money, certainly. As I'm sure you're aware, Ms. Gabriel," he said, directing his dark-blue gaze directly at her like a laser pointer and lowering his voice as though there were a complicit understanding between them, "There is unfortunately a very lucrative black market in antiquities, here and especially at Las Cruces near the Mexican border. Many a private collector would pay a great deal for the Oñate vessel. It might be sold from a middle-man to a private collector and never surface again for 50 years. Dorothea could have been part of a robbery gone wrong. Or had herself attacked to avert suspicion."

"From your perspective, Dr. Franchot, what is the special significance of this particular ceramic piece?"

"First, it's very old. It comes from the turn of the millennium, approximately 1000 A.D. Then, it has special markings on it probably denoting astronomical occurrences—shooting stars and the like. And, of course you know Don Juan de Oñate, the first Spanish conquistador to follow the Rio Grande up from what was new Spain all the way to Santa Fe. His signature is said to be engraved with a knife on the bottom, dating its use to around 1607, and being one of only two markings on artifacts possibly by Oñate's hand. The other one's carved on a rock in El Morro. I'm dubious about both of these so-called signatures, if you ask me, but Ned can undoubtedly give you a more learned explanation," he ended with evident distaste.

"And where were you, Dr. Franchot, at 4:30 p.m. today when we believe that attack on Ms. Yahouti occurred?"

"I was alone in my rooms writing." He stared directly into Officer Gabriel's gaze. "No one can vouch for me that I know of," he added with a smile, "except that I always write in my rooms in late afternoon before sherry and the evening meal in the great hall." I swear that he made the last words sound like a dinner invitation rather than an alibi, and Officer Gabriel reddened becomingly again.

"And you would have no objections if we search your rooms tonight?"

"It would be my pleasure," said Terry with a small leer. I rolled my eyes towards E.J. as if to question whether this was a police investigation or a dating service.

Officer Gabriel pulled herself together again and straightened her uniform. "Thank you, Dr. Franchot," she said with dignity. "My men and I will be up shortly." Terry stood up and shook her hand, holding it a little too long—his signature move, I noted—then nodded to E.J. and me, and walked up the stairs and out the door. Thank goodness that such crude maneuvers as the hand kiss are only allowed in France and not to individuals who insisted on pronouncing their last names as though they were in France.

Ned Gardner came in next and nodded courteously to the three of us before sitting down. How appropriate, I thought, for a serious occasion. No grandstanding, no cut-rate seduction techniques. Ned sank into one of the leather chairs with lanky ease, his legs crossed elegantly, his arms resting on the chair arms. Okay, okay, so I was more susceptible to his lower-key charm. Well-brought up and courteous in these and surely any circumstances, he offered to fill our glasses and I accepted another large quantity of water. It slid down effortlessly at this altitude whereas back in Washington, I had dutifully to drink the recommended eight glasses with difficulty, bribing myself with flavorings and colorings whenever possible.

Office Gabriel took Ned through the same paces, but without quite so much personal interest in his answers. On questioning, Ned said that he had been working in his office this afternoon when he heard a disturbance outside the larger of the two vaults. He ignored the sounds for a few minutes, but they got louder, and he went out to see what was happening. He found Dorothea on the ground, the key to the vault and a knife next to her hand. After speaking to her and trying to revive her, he ran back to his office and called 911. Yes, he had noted blood on the ground but did not see where it was coming from. No, he saw no one leaving the scene. He thought it might have taken him three or four minutes to get to Dorothea, not realizing at first that something serious was amiss. And yes, he had complete faith in her as a person and a professional.

"E.J. and I agreed, when I took this position last May, that her aunts would not have wanted the treasures that they had collected to be enjoyed exclusively by scholars—and that they would have wanted them to be understood, not only as historical objects of great beauty, but living objects with continuing meaning and resonance in the Indian cultures today. That's how we came up with the idea of the Native American docents, who could place these treasures in their sacred or non-sacred daily context. And we planned for greater access, not less, in the years ahead, for all kinds of visitors who wanted to learn." He paused. "Of course, safe-keeping of the collections is always the first priority—although not the only one." He shook his head sadly. "I am mortified that this happened under my watch, especially the violence to Ms. Yahouti. Do you have any news of her?"

Officer Gabriel replied: "She's still unconscious. Under guard at the hospital."

Ned's gray-tinged complexion grew a little grayer.

"Now, Mr. Gardner, when you first came to see Ms. Lowell (she checked her notes) last Monday, you discussed Dorothea's fears that someone had tampered with the glass case protecting the Oñate vessel. Can you tell me exactly what her words were?" Officer Gabriel was considerably more businesslike with Ned than she had been with Terry.

"Well, now that you mention it, what she actually said was that she had a feeling that someone had removed the shatterproof glass box on top of the artifact and that it seemed very slightly adjusted. In order to do that, someone would have had to turn off the electric switch first, but then nearly everyone here would have known how to do that," he concluded lamely. "I discussed this with E.J. but told no one else. E.J.," he continued, turning to her, "I'm terribly sorry for all this. It's entirely my fault."

E.J. sighed and shook her head. "Of course not, Ned."

Officer Gabriel stood up abruptly. "Thank you, Dr. Gardner. We'll be talking again soon. I'll hope you'll stay on or near the premises so that I can reach you easily if I have more questions."

We three followed Officer Gabriel out of E.J.'s office. The lesser officers had secured the crime scene and seemed to be doing a respectable job of collecting evidence. Officer Gabriel said a few words to her detectives, and with a whoosh of her shiny ponytail, she was gone.

E.J. looked exhausted for once. She asked Ned if he would show me to my room. She gave me a hug and said that she was glad I was here.

Ned and I left the main building and walked in the quiet dark along a path between the buildings of the center, illuminated only by a few sparse lights from several windows. We walked in silence for a few beats, hearing our footsteps against the stone paths. Ned looked slumped, defeated and naturally my heart went out to him.

"Thank you for showing me to my room," I said, just to make contact. "It must be awful for you to have this theft and the injury to Dorothea."

Ned was silent. "Thefts in the art world are more common than people know. But violence, to an innocent, kind woman—that's unacceptable."

His voice grew darker. "I'll never forgive myself for this."

I couldn't help wondering why Ned felt so particularly responsible. Without my asking, he seemed to answer me.

"I brought Dorothea here. I trained her, and she trained me. I taught her archeological book learning; she taught me how her Pueblo relatives still use these objects every day, and they still retain their sacred meaning. If I hadn't brought her here, this never would have happened."

We walked on for a bit, I noting my breath in the cold air as we moved along. Farther from the main administrative building and the great hall, it was quieter and a little eerie. Unexpectedly we came to the end of a path and directly to the low metal gates of a small well-kept cemetery. It had a weeping willow tree, two large crosses side by side marking graves, and about 12 smaller crosses in a semi-circle marking smaller graves. It looked like something from a Stephen King novel. This had to be a Native American burial ground (really bad karma) or a graveyard for slaughtered innocents.

Again, as though he could read my mind, Ned gave a short laugh at what must have been my shocked expression. "The Lowell sisters, Miranda and Philomena, are buried here. Along with every one of their beloved parakeets. Didn't E.J. tell you the story? Her aunts were traveling from Connecticut to California to winter in better weather with their pets, and stopped for birdseed in Santa Fe. They liked Santa Fe so much that they never left." He smiled sadly down at me. "It doesn't look so sinister in the daylight. The parakeet's names are on each of the crosses—Darwin, Maria Callas, Robespierre, Collette—I can't remember them all." I smiled back at him and liked him even better. "Of course, you saw their ceramic statues on the big desk in E.J.'s office."

"You know," he continued, as we rounded the corner to my two-story adobe Fellows' residence, "your first full day at the center shouldn't be completely ruined. Why don't I pick you up for breakfast at 7 o'clock tomorrow, and I'll show you the town in the patented Santa Fe early morning light? It's beautiful."

"I'd like that," I said, even though 7 a.m. sounded about ten minutes away. "But I have to be back by 9 o'clock for a tour of the center with Terry—"

Ned gave an involuntary snort at Terry's name, signaling no love lost.

"—and then I'm going with E.J. to San Juan Pueblo to see whether we can notify Dorothea's husband."

Ned opened the front door (nothing here was locked) and led me upstairs to a beautiful wooden door with a ceramic tile plate on it that read "The Roost."

"That's just metaphorical, right, Ned? None of your actual birds here? Because, come to think of it, I don't really like birds, dead or alive."

Ned laughed that inexplicably melancholy laugh that said he didn't have a right to, but did it anyway.

"No birds," he said. "Maybe just the ghosts of birds."

I shivered as I shut the door and threw myself fully clothed on the beautiful Spanish mission-style bed.

CHAPTER 8

"Of course the first thing to do was to make a grand survey of the country she was going to travel through."

—*Alice* Through the Looking Glass

I HAD JUST ENOUGH TIME to splash water on my face and change into one of my new Santa Fe outfits, the tan boots, the black gaucho jacket, the black pants, and the turquoise blouse, when I heard the expected knock on the door of the building downstairs.

I found myself running down the stairs with anticipation only to find not only Ned but E.J. there as well. We stood blinking at each other wordlessly in the strong morning sunlight.

"Sorry to interrupt your little twosome, Schaeff. We need to get going, but we thought you needed a few hours to sleep off that jet lag."

"No one else has been hurt, I hope."

"No," E.J. said, "But there's always the prospect of physical damage to me when the Aged Parents get wind of this disaster."

"I like how you look on the bright side, E.J.," I said.

E.J. passed the conversational ball to Ned with a nod, and he began reluctantly, "Well, after I dropped you off last night, Schaeffer," (he said my name a little softly, like a caress), "I went back to E.J.'s office and we opened the vaults for Officer Gabriel's inspection. The first vault has the weavings, mostly Navajo. It looked fine. The second vault has basketry and pots, the pots being among the most ancient, rare and valuable in the country. Most of them are on floor-to-ceiling shelves. We remove them only for scholarly use, for conservation, and for a very occasional loan to a museum. But a very few are on display, in glass cases, so that they may be easily seen when we have tours."

"This isn't a freshman lecture, Ned. Less preamble, more point."

Ned gave a grim smile and continued on methodically. "Then we went to the first vault, to see where the Oñate vessel had been before it was stolen. Clearly it was one of our most valuable objects. The aunts had acquired it, but we, I really, discovered it in what we call the attic, a room filled with a jumble of un-catalogued, unidentified and odd items. It turned out to be something extremely unusual—"

"All right. Let's go to breakfast," E.J. said. "I may faint before you get to the point."

We walked a few yards to the green Subaru and climbed in.

Ned continued, "Let me describe it to you. It's a rather small pottery cup, you can hold it in the palm of your hand. It's not very ornate, but it's very old, circa A.D. 1100 to 1300, the height of the Pueblo civilization in the area. You know that the Pueblo Indians have been living in this part of the world for thousands of years—they say they came out of the earth here—and settled in villages along the Rio Grande and even in the desert. These ancient Pueblo peoples, named "Anasazi" by their enemies the Navajo, created the great cliff dwellings, Chaco Canyon to the West and Canon de Chelly, farther north. They were huge—some of the "Great Houses" had over 600 rooms and dozens of kiwas, or ceremonial spaces. They traded far and wide—we've found sea shells from the west coast and parrot feathers from Mexico."

While Ned talked, I was lulled by his soft voice and the pictures he was drawing in words. E.J. drove madly through Santa Fe, and in about five minutes we had squeezed into a parking space in front of a tiny store front on San Francisco Street, and were entering a breakfast place called Tia Sophia. We were seated by a friendly waiter, who was probably a concert cellist, and ordered *huevos rancheros*, a kind of Tex-Mex omelet, and some very strong coffee. I also ordered a Mexican hot chocolate.

"So when I saw this small cup, made of clay, I recognized it at once as a very old piece of pottery, dating from around 1200 A.D. But what made it special—no, extraordinary—was that it had a complex pictogram scratched on the sides of it, reminiscent of the petroglyphs, the writing scratched into walls, that were found in the ancient dwellings of Chaco Canyon."

"What was it a picture of?" I asked between bites.

"No one agrees on that. Ancient Pueblo writing and drawing has never been adequately deciphered. There are many theories. This picture, a circle, a figure and a spiraling star shape, could be something astrological, but it could also be a sign for different clans merging, or an explanation of what happened to make the ancient Pueblos abandon their homes and move further east and south. So much is still a mystery."

"Exactly my point, Ned," E.J. interrupted impatiently.

"Wait, but there's more," Ned said with a rueful glance. "Scratched on the bottom of this otherwise unadorned cup, very, very faintly, is what appears to be an amazing signature: that of Don Juan de Oñate, the first and arguably the cruelest conquistador that ever tried to conquer this region—"

"And the Pueblo Indians with them—" E.J. added.

"For Spain. It's one of the first pieces we have that testifies to interconnections between Spanish and Indian cultures in this region."

"And this is the cup that we found missing in the vaults after the attack on Dorothea." E.J. concluded. "This little cup, probably the only one like it in the whole world, which is the pride of my aunts' collection, and was soon to be written up in the *National Geographic*, for heaven's sake—secure in its little glass box on its neat little pedestal, with mirrors over and under so that you could see the Indian pictures in the cup and the probably authentic Oñate signature scratched on the bottom—was *gone*! Missing! Vanished!"

I told E.J. that I had managed to get the picture. "And I suppose there were no prints on the glass? Or the door to the vault? Or the key to the vault, other than the ones we'd expect to find."

"I don't think so," E.J. said glumly. "Officer Gabriel sent us out and tested for 'latent' prints, whatever they are."

I hoped that Officer Gabriel had been thorough. Latent prints could be on anything where a finger had touched any surface, as long as the moisture of sweat or bodily oils remained or could be reawakened from the surface. Modern testing had many tools at its disposal—ultra violet light, etc. etc., far from the early days of merely spreading talcum powder over everything and hoping to see a large perfect thumbprint emerge. I had a small fingerprinting kit with me, and planned to do my own testing if Officer Gabriel didn't turn anything up.

"But she didn't expect to find any," E.J. continued. "She said that any prints would probably have been made by people at the center, which wouldn't prove anything. And a professional thief would have worn gloves."

"Let me get this straight, E.J.," I said. "After Ned made this amazing discovery, you've managed in a few short months to lose a historic piece of pottery that not only has immense value to scholars and is worth a great deal of money to collectors, but that also has special significance both to the Pueblo peoples as a living part of their ancient culture and to Hispanics, who tend to overlook Oñate's cruelty and focus on his historical significance?"

"You could put it that way," E.J. said gloomily. "You sound a good deal like Moms and Pater will sound if we don't get it back."

I looked up in time to catch Ned's sympathetic gaze before I saw a dark shadow cover our table and block out the cheery morning sunlight.

CHAPTER 9

"Dear Bathurst...was a man to my very heart's content: he hated a fool, and he hated a rogue, and he hated a Whig; he was a very good hater."

—Dr. Johnson

"**I** thought I'd find you here, Elizabeth Jane," said a tall man dressed all in black including a black cape and military style beret.

The speaker was a handsome but harsh looking man in his sixties with an aquiline nose, chiseled features and black hair streaked with silver.

"Good morning, to you, too, Philip," E.J. replied with annoyance. I noted that the intruder carefully eschewed the nickname E.J., which everyone else used. "You know Ned Gardner, of course, and this is Schaeffer Cornell. Schaeffer, this is Commander Philip Gomez-Ibañes."

The commander gave us the briefest of nods and tapped his silver tipped black cane on the tile floor impatiently.

"As Chairman of the Board of Trustees of the center, I would have thought that I would have heard from you by now, and not have to rely on one of your underlings, Mr. Franchot. I need to talk with you in my office. Now."

"I'm afraid that will have to wait, Philip. I'm on my way to see Dorothea Yahouti in the hospital now. Surely you heard about her condition, as well as the stolen vessel. I still value human life over pottery, no matter how rare."

"Very well," Mr. Gomez-Ibañes said. "I suppose you'll want Ned with you. I always opposed the idea of Native docents, as you know. This is just the sort of sloppy, bad handling of historical treasures that occurs when you leave matters in their hands."

E.J. sighed, deciding that resistance was futile.

"I'll see you at my offices in the Palace at 10 o'clock sharp," Philip Gomez-Ibañes continued.

"We'll try," said E.J. "And since you haven't asked, Schaeffer Cornell is a college friend, artist, and new fellow at the center. She arrived yesterday."

"Auspicious timing," Frank said, extending the tips of his fingers on a well-manicured hand. "Why don't I take Ms. Cornell with me to the Palace and give her a private tour. You can meet her at 10 o'clock as planned."

I gave a quick glance at E.J. and she nodded for me to go with Philip. I was being held hostage, I knew, but I also would get to learn more about Philip in his natural habitat. The more you know, the more you can know, I thought to myself, and followed El Commandante out the door.

Philip kept up a brisk military pace on foot as I struggled to keep up with him in my new Santa Fe boots. We turned two short corners and up on my right came the unexpected and wonderful view of the Santa Fe Plaza, a grassy rectangle criss-crossed with paths, ringed on all sides with two-story adobe buildings. Within the plaza, scattered throughout on the grass, were wrought-iron benches, anchored by a painted white gazebo at the center. It was amazingly like the Zocalo square in Oaxaca, Mexico. I had never seen anything so perfectly foreign in the old U.S. of A. For the first time, I began to understand viscerally that North America was not colonized only by pale-complected Congregationalists. My eyes widened and I silently blamed Mrs. Heilbut, my fourth grade teacher, for talking about pilgrims ad nauseum and omitting this other essential part of our history. The plaza was very small really—a city block on each side—and delightfully charming and animated, even today on a cool, early morning in March that seemed to threaten snow.

Philip said little until we reached "The Palace of the Governors," which in spite of its grand name was a low-slung adobe affair, one-story high, that occupied the whole north end of the Plaza. It was not unlike the other adobe buildings on the other sides of the square except that it had a very large wooden door in front. Like most adobe buildings, it had vigas—large, ex-posed beams jutting out from the roof—that supported a permanent awning that ran the whole length of the building. Cinderella's Castle at Disneyland it was not. Nor the White House, nor even a McMansion in McLean, Virginia. But it had its own low-key grandeur. Philip informed me that the structure was 400 years old and the oldest public building in the nation.

In front of the Palace, as we got nearer, I could see rows of Native Americans sitting cross-legged on blankets or more comfortably on deck-chairs, leaning against the front wall under the awning and displaying fine jewelry in turquoise and silver. I knew from my guidebook that this was the Indian-run cooperative market, where Indians could display and sell their handiwork daily, that all had to be handmade and signed by the artist, and that if too many sellers showed up, a lottery for space was held. My eyes were drawn to a particularly lovely silver necklace imbedded with turquoise stones, but Philip didn't let me pause. He opened the front wooden door and ushered me almost roughly inside.

"Indians," he said under his breath. "Always underfoot." To me he added, "They really ruin the vista of the Palace from the plaza. They obscure the simple, unadorned, and authentic architecture of the Palace that we all prize."

He walked me past the front entry desk waving dismissively to the ticket seller and continued, "We did, of course, have the front façade fully cleaned and cleared in 1998, for the 400th Anniversary (Quatro Centenario) of the Founding of the Spanish colony in New Mexico by Don Juan de Oñate in 1598. Former Spanish Vice-President Francisco Alvarez-Cascos presented six replica 17th-century military uniforms and accoutrements as part of the Spanish nation's gift to us."

I stared at Philip Gomez-Ibañes as he poured out this information like a tour guide who had memorized his part. And yet, to be fair, Philip Gomez-Ibañes repeated these words with feeling, a glassy-eyed nostalgia creeping onto his face. I was just beginning to realize just how closely Philip Gomez-Ibañes identified with his heritage from Spain, when I was about to be hit with more reminiscences.

"Yes, I carried the purple banner, a reproduction of the processional banner carried by Commander Don Juan de Oñate himself in 1598. The banner now hangs in my office."

And he guided me along a wooden corridor, which sometimes widened into wooden rooms, each filled with small exhibits of 16th- and 17th-century items. These rooms and corridors enclosed a central rectangular yard, which one could see through the windows, with a well in its center. It was in the form of all the Spanish-style missions and military presideos that I had seen in California.

Finally, Philip led me through one room with a glass case, bearing a saddle, with golden filigree peeling off, silver plates and bowls and some earthenware pots and cups.

"These are examples of period wares," he began calmly and then suddenly, wrought himself into fury. "THIS is where Don Juan de Oñate's vessel would be today—if it hadn't been for that nouveau-arriviste Elizabeth Jane Lowell and her amateur Indian friends." Calming himself down, he led me into his office, which featured, as promised, the replica of Don Juan de Oñate's purple banner, done in elegant silk. In another case by a simple wooden desk, was certainly one of the six uniforms that made up part of the gift from Spain.

I looked around his office as we sat down and he attended to some notes on his desk. Besides the mementos of Colonial Spain, the room contained some mesmerizing examples of religious art. One depiction of Christ on the Cross was particularly disturbing. It was beautifully carved and extraordinarily detailed, but the extreme pain and anguish of the twisted figure was like a punch in the stomach, and the painted blood gushing from every wound made me want to look away.

Philip must have read my thoughts.

"Yes, that is a unique and extraordinary piece of Hispanic folk art, carved by a santero—a sculptor of religious icons—who was also a Brother of the Penitentes. It's a Spanish Catholic sect that experiences Christ through emulating his suffering for mankind. Don Juan de Oñate was a Brother of the Penitentes. He is said to have celebrated his first Good Friday in the New World somewhere just south of El Paso with scourging and self-flagellation."

I must have looked horrified, as he continued, "But, of course, the Penitentes have been outlawed now. Excommunicated from the Catholic Church.

"It is fashionable," he added calmly, as we sat facing each other across his desk, "to make light of or dismiss, or even denigrate the Spanish legacy of New Mexico. It is considered, for some reason, snobbish to trace one's ancestors back to the Conquistadors, who first claimed New Mexico for Spain. Do you, for example, look down on easterners who are proud to be descended from the intrepid colonists who came on the Mayflower?"

I decided not to answer that directly. I could trace my ancestors back only about two generations and knew little about them. Thus, it had instinctively been my practice not to award any extra points to individuals for their lineage or pedigree.

"But Don Juan de Oñate, if I may say so, and his followers, have a reputation for cruelty."

"Ah, these were cruel times. No one blames the Mayans or Aztecs for beheading their victims."

"But the Pueblo Indians, who lived in the Rio Grande Valley before Oñate came, as I understand it, were peaceable folks, farmers, or so I've heard."

"The Pueblos were nothing! They had nothing—no horses, no tools, no culture—only corn, maize, everywhere. No civilization to speak of."

I looked appalled but said nothing.

"Everyone in New Mexico is so mixed anyway, today," he continued, "Indian and Mexican, Anglo and Jew, there are so few who—like me—can trace our ancestry back clearly and purely.

"Only we, the members of La Orden Militar de los Descendiantes de los Primeros Soldatos—Pobladores y Conquistadors—are allowed the honor of wearing these uniforms. I am proud to have carried Don Juan de Oñate's banner and to have worn the uniform of the Conquistadors!" Although he included a lot of Spanish words that I couldn't understand, I think I got the picture. He paused, and looked at me directly, "And from what stock do you descend, my dear?" He added with an attempt at kind condescension.

This was a bit of a puzzling question, seeing that I was currently undercover as the great niece of the famous artist Joseph Cornell. Rather than alluding to my fictitious ancestry, of which I really hadn't a clue, I took the opportunity to alienate Mr. Gomez-Ibañes further—there really was no other choice: "I come from people who put little stock in where a person comes from but rather in what he does with his life."

Chew on that, Mr. Conquistador, I thought with pleasure, while I feigned a vigorous interest in my fingernails.

Our tête-à-tête, thank heaven, was interrupted on this happy note by the arrival of E.J. and Ned, who knocked and then burst into the room.

Philip Gomez-Ibañes stood up and questioned loudly, "The Oñate cup?" just as E.J. announced simultaneously "Dorothea—"

Philip fell silent.

"Dorothea is dead," said E.J. as she sat heavily in the chair that Ned quickly provided.

CHAPTER 10

"The first step toward tolerance is respect, and the first step toward respect is knowledge."

—*Henry Louis Gates, Jr.*

"**W**ELL," SAID PHILIP IMPATIENTLY. "What are you going to do about it?"

"I'm going to San Juan Pueblo to notify Dorothea's next of kin."

"You know what I meant," he said coldly. "Because I know what I'm going to do. I'm going to call a meeting of the board and have you and Ned fired for incompetence.

"Do you realize that apart from one signature carved into the rock of El Morro in 1605 with the words *Pasó por aqui*—'I passed here'—this is the only extant signature of the man in New Mexico? There are a thousand pots—there are thousands of Indians—but there are only two signatures of Senior Don Juan de Oñate, and I want the one we had back!"

"You do what you have to do," E.J. said just as freshly. "Schaeffer and I will find your darned Oñate vessel, Philip, and I just hope we do before anyone else gets killed over it."

Philip was silent. Ned looked at me uncertainly. I shrugged.

Fighting off tears, E.J. walked out of the room, and Ned and I followed. We saw Philip picking up the telephone as we left.

"I'm so sorry about Dorothea," I said, putting my arm around E.J. as we walked. She allowed a few tears to drip down her ruddy cheeks, and then sniffed loudly into her tissue.

"I feel responsible," she said. "What do I know about running a research center? My parents are right. I'm a ne'er-do-well who should be spending time her time wearing lime green and perfecting my golf swing at a country club somewhere."

"That's not true," Ned said. "You've done a good job. No one could have prevented what happened. Anyhow, it's my fault," he said bitterly.

"You know," I said, trying to be helpful, "the difference between everything being all right and nothing being right and everyone's life shattered, is a really fine line." They both looked at me resentfully, further depressed by my philosophy of life, so I tried another tack.

"Hey, you guys. Stop flagellating yourselves. Bad things happen all the time. Besides, we have a lot of work to do." We climbed back into the Subaru. "Did you see Officer Gabriel? Will she report on the autopsy results?" I asked.

"Yes. And she's keeping the loss of the clay vessel to herself. She wants to hold that in reserve. In fact, she's keeping everything quiet for now."

E.J. slowly began reviving and assuming her usual authority. True grit will win out, I thought to myself.

"Ned, I'll call Terry Franchot at the center. Let him call a meeting with the fellows and tell them about Dorothea. He certainly seems eager to spread bad news. I need you both with me when we visit Dot's family."

And with that she had a short conversation on her cell phone, and turned the car north toward the outskirts of Santa Fe, along Highway 68 toward San Juan Pueblo.

The road followed the Rio Grande up toward Tesuque Pueblo, and then through the little town of Españiola, famous for its low-rider cars, that is, souped-up 1950s and '60s vehicles, often convertibles, with colorful and distinctive decorations and original paint jobs, driven by souped-up looking young people.

Along the way, the land was parched. Elusive clouds billowed up prettily, but did not even suggest a rainstorm. Every once in a while, we saw a garage or a gas station. Finally we came to the Ohkay Casino, my first experience with an Indian-owned gambling den. It was small and tasteful, and next to it was a small Ramada Inn. We went inside briefly and found it quiet and pretty wholesome. The volume of the slot machines was turned low and the lights were bright. Waitresses, dressed in non-skimpy outfits, circulated with trays of brightly colored soft drinks. A bingo room at the side attracted older customers. Everyone in the place looked Indian. The gift shop, though, was filled with kitsch—little Indian-dolls with big eyes, made in China.

The foyer had pictures of the Governor of the Pueblo and the Tribal elders as well as a small glass-enclosed stature of Po'Pay (Ripe Pumpkin), 16th-century leader of a successful Pueblo revolt against the Spaniards, and a native son of San Juan Pueblo. The Pueblo Indians were even able to take over the Palace of the Governors in 1680 until it was retaken by the Spaniards 11 years later. Under the small statue of Po'Pay was a collection box to erect a life-size statue of him in San Juan Pueblo.

After this break, we took a left on a side road off the highway to the center of San Juan Pueblo. Like any Native American reservation, this Pueblo was a Sovereign Nation, subject to its own laws, presided over by a governor, elected for one or two years, a council of tribal elders, its own judiciary, and a police force. The road to the Pueblo was well paved, neat and rather cozy houses appeared on both sides. A sign pointed to the Community School, and another to the center of the Pueblo.

The town center was dusty but well maintained. We parked in front of a complex of small, one-story adobe buildings, which included a door with a plaque saying "Governor's Office." E.J. knocked and we were let in by the Deputy Governor, a small, neat man in khakis and a collared shirt. A large deputy's badge attached to the collar. He told us that the Governor would be back from his job in Los Alamos shortly and that we could wait in the adjacent crafts cooperative.

There a handsome young woman and an older woman were beading necklaces at a kitchen table. Unlike at the Casino Shop, the crafts here were authentic and Indian-made, in both traditional and contemporary styles. E.J. urged me to augment my accessory collection and suggested I buy a necklace of seeds and dried beans. Not wanting to be pecked to death by hungry pigeons, however, I bought a beautiful turquoise choker of intricately strung beads instead. Ned offered to help me with the clasp, and I felt his nearness and a hint of his breath on my neck. What was I thinking?

Soon the Governor greeted us, and led us in to his well-appointed inner office. Among the many pictures on the walls, in a place of honor, were two crossed ceremonial scepters, which the Governor later explained were given by Abraham Lincoln to each of the Pueblo Governors as a re-dedication to the sovereignty of the Pueblo nations, and were crossed with a similar piece delivered by the government of Spain. On his wall, too, were portraits of the tribal elders, none of them women, I was sorry to note. The Governor shook hands with each of us. He was a very large and capable looking man, threatening when his face was serious, warm and kindly-looking when he smiled a toothy smile. E.J. introduced us and thanked him for seeing us and thanked his deputy for taking such good care of us.

"My deputy is a good man," said the Governor. "He is my right-hand man." He paused and smiled again. "Of course, I have to say that. He is my first cousin."

I began to see how close knit this community was. Dorothea was bound to be related to someone here, and her death, I thought, would be taken hard.

E.J. spoke again after these greetings. "We are here with very sad news, Governor," she said. "Dorothea Yahouti, who has worked with me and my colleagues at the research center in Santa Fe for the last year, was injured fatally yesterday. We don't know who did it."

The Governor was stunned silent. Finally, he said, "Dorothea is my cousin, too."

We sat in silence until he spoke again and asked for the details, which Ned filled in, including the missing pot with the Oñate signature and the Ancient Pueblo symbols on the sides.

"I'll find these despicable men," said the Governor, with force, and then more softly, "If only I'd have persuaded her to stay on here. But she wanted to go and teach others about the ancient Pueblo arts. She was proud of her heritage. There are many ways to serve."

Silence again.

Finally, E.J. cleared her throat and began. "Governor, is Dorothea's husband here so that I can break the news to him?"

The Governor used his intercom to speak in Tewa to his deputy.

"The deputy will check."

As we waited in silence Ned asked, "Do you know anyone who could have done this?"

"Art thieves are everywhere. This piece that you describe has importance to our people and the Spanish descendants who worship that devil Oñate." The intercom buzzer cut him off. The Deputy Governor entered quickly. "Simon is probably in the desert on one of his archeological surveys. No one has seen him for two days, but I found this in his and Dorothea's room."

He handed the Governor a piece of notepaper. The Governor read it, shook his head and handed it to E.J., who shared it with Ned and me.

It was dated yesterday and it said, "Forgive me, Dorothea. I have to do this. Simon."

We sat in silence and tried to take in this message. What had Simon had to do? Why would Dorothea have to forgive him? Where was he now?

And how could we find him?

The Governor supplied some information. "Simon is a Hopi on his father's side and has a part-time job in Gallup to the west. He's Acoma Pueblo on his mother's side. He is trained as an archaeo-astronomer and he believes that the ancient Pueblos left great knowledge of astronomy in archeological symbols. Simon spends weeks in the desert at a time searching for these discoveries, often at the ruins of Chaco Canyon."

"Governor," I said, "Do you think that Simon could have stolen the vessel? Surely he couldn't have hurt Dorothea. And why do you think Dorothea's attackers slit her right ankle?"

"Ah," said the Governor thoughtfully. "I cannot believe that Simon would hurt Dorothea. But what he would do for his research is another matter. The knife wound in Dorothea's ankle—that's a reference to Oñate's torture of the people of Acoma Pueblo. When the Acoma people threw some of Oñate's army off their land into the valley below, Oñate retaliated by taking all of their women and children and selling them into slavery and cutting off the right foot of every able-bodied man."

"How horrible," I said.

"If you go up to the Don Juan de Oñate Memorial just a little north of here, you'll see a great brute of a statue of Oñate on horseback. As soon as it was put up, some people came and sawed off the statue's right foot. Of course, the people at the Memorial only soldered it back on again. But it was worth doing. Surprisingly, the perpetrators were not found..."

"So you think Dorothea's attackers were identifying themselves...as Oñate's descendants?"

"Could be," said the Governor thoughtfully. "But why would they leave a signature to the crime?"

"Or maybe that they were leaving a message about Acoma Pueblo?"

The Governor shrugged.

"Do you know where we should start looking for Simon?" I asked.

The Governor shrugged again, "Maybe in Gallup, or at his mother's house in Acoma Pueblo, or maybe in Chaco Canyon–"

"But that's vast," said E.J., "and nearly impassable this time of year, either from mud or ice."

I had a thought then and turned to Ned. "Do you remember the symbols etched into the sides of the pot? Can you recreate them?"

"Of course," Ned said, speaking for the first time.

The Governor offered him a piece of paper and a pen and he drew the following: an exploding star, a spiral, a man, and a comet.

"Does this mean anything to you, Governor?" I asked.

"Everyone reads the ancient petroglyphs differently. I see nebulae, perhaps the Pueblo of Acoma to the South, and possibly a cross."

"Thank you," I said, thinking to myself of Polonius's changeable identification of clouds, "and very like a whale." Petroglyph interpretation was clearly an art rather than a science.

"This is just the sort of symbol that Simon is so intent on finding and interpreting," the Governor continued.

Simon? The missing vessel? Could he have taken it?

E.J. and the Governor then spoke quietly about bringing his cousin Dorothea Yahouti back home for burial. Ned and I compared notes.

"It sounds to me as though we need to find Simon. Maybe he even has the vessel in question. He's pretty dedicated to his research—scarily so—I sometimes think," Ned suggested.

"If Simon has it, we just need to find him before the thugs do. I can't believe that Simon could attack his own wife."

"Of course not. I know him. He often came for the day with Dorothea. He's a wonderful man, just a little tunnel-visioned when it comes to his work. I've been there."

E.J. joined us after a few minutes. "Let's go back and think about our next steps," she said. She checked her cell phone for messages and turned to us with a sigh. "Oh rats and mice," she said. "Another trustee of the center, Veronica Rutherford, is waiting for me and Ned up at her house in Bishop's Lodge. Might as well stop by on the way back and get yelled at. Better to have it over all at once."

"Can we see the Oñate statue on the way back?"

"It's actually a few minutes north, but okay. Best you know the cultural lay of the land."

Well, the great Oñate was memorialized with a fine equestrian bronze statue right near the road on Route 68. He looked every inch the conquistador, spurs flashing, a whip in his right hand. Sure enough, the right foot of the statue had once been sawed off at the ankle and just as clearly someone else had lovingly repaired it, making it almost good as new. "The past is not dead," William Faulkner wrote, "It is not even past." Of course, he was writing about the South, in his mind a swamp of incest and slavery soup. But I was beginning to think that the Southwest, here, could give Faulkner's South a run for its money.

After a short and uninspiring stop at the statue, we turned around and headed south to Santa Fe, stopping for a snack at the Tesuque market, an informal eatery with a lovely outside porch (too cold) and a cramped restaurant strung with colored lights in the shape of chile peppers, red and green. The food was delicious—chiles rellenos and rice and beans with cold Mexican Tecate beer.

We ate quickly and didn't talk much though. We finished, paid up, and drove a little farther south to the outskirts of Santa Fe, and east into the foothills of the Sangre de Cristo Mountains. We passed the Santa Fe Opera House, a strange and arresting outdoor arena looking a little like the Sidney Opera House with its sails to the wind.

At Bishop's Gate Lodge Road, we took a sharp left and came up against a large and impenetrable wall—the entry to the gated community where Veronica Rutherford lived. After several ill-timed attempts to buzz us through, the walls eventually parted and we starting driving up a winding gravel path with large adobe style houses every acre or so. Near the very top of this hill, we turned up a dirt road to Veronica's homestead, and the old Subaru began to baulk.

"There, there," said E.J. soothingly to her car. "You've done enough for one day. Let's get out and walk, you guys."

I thought we'd been through a lot today, too, but I guess I didn't have as many miles on me as E.J.'s trusty old Subaru. The three of us trudged up about a half mile of gravel drive. I would have complained except that the sky of layered clouds was creating the most beautiful sunset I'd yet seen over the Sangre de Cristo Mountains, blood red, deep violet. I could see why the mountains were called Blood of Christ.

By the time we got to the front door of Veronica's house, the sun had set and a very light dry snow had begun to fall. Veronica's house was a soaring adobe with great glass windows on three sides. She greeted us somewhat petulantly as soon as we rang the bell, as though she had been lying in wait, ready to spring.

Actually, Veronica Rutherford was pretty tightly coiled up in general. She was a handsome widow "of a certain age" with a perfect oval face, narrow brown eyes and a mannish but becoming haircut. She was dressed all in black—turtleneck, jeans, cowboy boots, and ornamented only by a ring with a diamond as big as the Ritz and a turquoise necklace with stones the size of Texas.

"You're late, E.J.," she said curtly, acknowledging Ned and me with a nod. "Alicia had to leave, but she left something in the oven for us, I think. I only hope it isn't totally ruined."

She ushered us into a mile-high kitchen, the counter tops of rare white granite marble, the windows revealing outlines of the mountains still visible. The floor was of large, Mexican sienna tiles. On the wall was one very large piece of art. From a distance, it looked like a huge silver cross with a rough surface. Close-up, I could see that it was made of crushed Mexican beer cans and bottle tops. Veronica noticed my obvious admiration for what turned out to be her favorite art work and relaxed a little.

"I understand you are Joseph Cornell's great niece," she said.

News travels fast around Santa Fe, I realized.

"I've always admired his work. I like outsider art—the odd, untrained, or the slightly insane are so much more creative. I must have original art and ancient Pueblo pottery, right, Ned?" She spoke to him for the first time.

She reached into the oven and brought forth a huge mound of delicious-looking crab cakes, which must have been flown in from one coast or the other at enormous expense. She placed them on a ceramic plate on a rattan tray and had us follow her into the living room, a room even more beautiful than the kitchen, perhaps because of a great fireplace at its center, with a lusty fire ablaze. It smelled of hickory or something wonderful. And through large windows at both sides of the fire you could see the light snow falling onto a floodlit patio. The outside and inside barrier seemed to have been broken by the warmth of the fire and the cool of the snow.

Veronica sat in one maroon leather chair and E.J. took the other. I was happy to sit next to Ned on a low-slung and very comfortable maroon leather couch.

The glass coffee table in the center had been set for us with white wine, salad, and now the wonderful hot crab cakes. Ned poured for us and Veronica served in her impatient tightly coiled manner, and started eating immediately in a kind of rude insouciant way that only the very rich are allowed.

I raised my glass and toasted, "To the most beautiful house I've ever been in," and drank the glass of vibrant white wine. I felt better immediately.

"Now, E.J.," said Veronica, when she had eaten a good amount of the crab cake and salad and swilled a full glass of wine. "What's going on at the center? Philip Gomez-Ibañes has been telling me all sorts of horrid things about Dorothea being killed and your prized artifact stolen. Is that right? What will your parents say?"

"Nothing—if they don't know about it," said E.J. "What Philip told you is basically true. I'm sick about Dorothea. I can't bring myself to care as much about the pot—"

"So Philip told me—"

"And I'd be grateful if you'd allow me to sort this out—at least for a few days—before you communicate with Mother."

"Ned, what do you think?" said Veronica pointedly. "I do have a duty as a board member as well as an old friend of E.J.'s mother."

"Vanderbilt University, Phi Kappa Phi sorority," E.J. said to me in an audible aside. "Moms and Veronica are sorority sisters although, of course, Veronica attended Vanderbilt much later than Moms."

"And why hasn't it been in the papers, anyway?" Veronica demanded, not giving Ned a chance to reply, for which he seemed grateful.

"I've been wondering that myself, Veronica," E.J. said. "I pleaded with the officer on the case to keep it quiet, but I never expected that she would."

Ned said, "You know, Veronica, we do have a lead on where the Oñate vessel might be. We think that Dorothea's husband, Simon, might have taken it for some reason. He's an expert on Anasazi archaeo-astronomy. A weird duck who spends most of his time in the desert looking for signs that the Ancient Pueblo knew a great deal about astronomical phenomena. The sides of this ancient pot—and it might be as old as the first century A.D.—have some pretty significant looking new markings—reminiscent of the ones found at Chaco Canyon."

"And what about the Oñate signature etched in the bottom? I don't think it's a coincidence that Oñate owned the vessel. He must have understood its significance even in 1598. It's so unfortunate that no records have yet been found but," she turned to me, "as you may not know, the Pueblo Indians, led by Po'Pay of San Juan Pueblo, burned the whole Palace of the Governor's down, with all of its records, in 1680. To this day, I can't forgive them for that destruction. It was built up again of course, but so much was destroyed."

"Yet you like your ancient pots, Veronica," said Ned, with what I thought was undue emphasis.

"Hmph," humphed Veronica. "Yes, the Pueblos did make magnificent pottery. Schaeffer, would you like to see my collection? Most of it is in New York, but I keep a few ceramics here."

She got up and I followed her to the right side of the room, which she illuminated with a switch of carefully directed track lighting. Suddenly three pedestals were lighted and displayed what to my untrained eye were pieces of extraordinary age and beauty.

"These are remarkable," I said.

"Yes," Veronica said simply. "It was much easier to acquire them some years ago when the law wasn't so stringent about selling antiques, Native Rights, and Repatriation Laws. It's all so silly. The pots should be where they'd be appreciated and preserved in good condition."

This seemed rather high-handed to me. But what about Veronica wasn't high-handed? Do you know the expression, 'more money than you know what to do with'?

"All right, you three. You have a lead on the pot in question, and you want some time to follow it before I turn you in to my sorority sister."

E.J. nodded gratefully.

"Would you also like some company?"

A stunned silence ensued. There was practically no way that our search would be made easier with the addition of Veronica Rutherford, Vanderbilt University, Phi Kappa Phi.

"Well, we'll be moving quickly," began Ned.

"And perhaps having to visit some rough places." E.J. continued hopefully.

"Nonsense," Veronica said. "I care about this pot as if it were my own."

"Don't you trust us?" said Ned.

"Not a whit," said Veronica, and there ended the discussion.

E.J. explained that our best lead so far was trying to find Dorothea's husband Simon. If we could find him, we might get a clue to the whereabouts of the missing vessel.

"Where do we start looking?" said Veronica with that same hungry intensity with which she addressed her crab cakes.

"I'm not sure," E.J. said. "Simon has a car and a day's start on us. He might have headed to place near Gallup or his mother's house in Acoma Pueblo. He might have gone to Chaco Canyon though how we'd find him in that vast place, I can't imagine. I say we start with Gallup."

I got out my map of New Mexico. "Can we stop at Acoma Pueblo first?" I said. "It's on the way."

"Acoma it is, then," E.J. said. "If you really need to go with us, Veronica, please be at the center at 7 o'clock tomorrow morning. You know it could be dangerous. The killer who murdered Dorothea might be looking for the pot, too."

"No matter," Veronica said.

"And they've already killed once," E.J. continued. "As they always say, 'they won't hesitate to kill again.'"

"Seven o'clock it is then," said Veronica drily. "And now let me see you out. Leave everything. Alicia will see to it in the morning."

"This is a nightmare," said E.J. as we trudged down the gravel path to our car.

"On top of a bad dream," Ned added. "As if we didn't have enough problems, we have Veronica on our backs and in our faces." Ned seemed even more distressed than E.J., if such a thing were possible.

"I'm going to stay at the center," E.J. decided. "You call in and keep me informed. I'm not going anywhere with that snobbish, Indian-hating witch."

"She and Philip Gomez-Ibañes seem to make a good pair," I observed. "Are they close?"

"Well, they're both snobs, but for different reasons, you know. Veronica is old money and Philip is old Spain. Veronica is an art collector of the most fanatical sort, and Philip is only out to preserve the history and glories of old Spain. Did he tell you how he got hold of the purple banner when the King of Spain visited Santa Fe in 1998—the Quincentenary of Don Juan de Oñate's first visit?"

"No, do tell," I said sarcastically.

"Oh," E.J. said. "He had you for five minutes so I should have known that he would have mentioned that. Did he tell you that he is a member of La Orden Militar de los Descendientes de los Primeros Soldados Pobladores y Conquistadores?"

"He may have," I answered, "but my attention was beginning to wane at that point. Also he said it in Spanish."

"This Military Order of the Descendants of the First Spanish Soldiers and Conquerors, is a somewhat sinister group of men who promote Spanish glories in New Mexico. They must be of pure Spanish blood, members of the Catholic faith, understand Spanish, and have a positive—nay, worshipful—commitment to the first Spanish Conquerors of New Mexico."

"Not a surprise," I said.

"It's a small, tightly knit and loyal group."

"So Philip and Veronica are not of one mind?"

"Only coincidentally. They both hate the Mexicans—that is, the non pure-blooded Spanish residents of Santa Fe—and the modern Indians as below contempt. But Philip gets to hate Anglos too, which puts him one up," Ned added.

"But Veronica is richer, which puts her one up," E.J. said. "Anyhow, they share notes and tend to vote together in the center's Board."

"At least we're not traveling with Philip," I said. "Veronica is marginally better."

"Six of one, half dozen of the other," said Ned as we pulled into the center.

As we made the turn, I noticed a car speeding on by, which may have been behind us for some time. Funny, now that I thought of it, it had been behind us all the way home. There were killers on the loose and I was losing my focus. I vowed to be more careful from then on.

CHAPTER 11

"If you're going to count your chickens, be sure to tag their toes."

—Gwendlyn Katz-Spielberg

SIX THIRTY A.M. THE NEXT MORNING found me awake and alert in the communal kitchen of the research center. I had packed a small bag and was just foraging for some breakfast-type nourishment, when Ned came and offered to make a pot of life-saving coffee. For my part, I found some butter and eggs, and began to scramble up a batch.

We sat across from each other at the wooden table, not talking much. I was savoring the coffee and eggs and the light streaking in on a small glass vase filled with violets. I looked up and smiled at Ned who was not eating much.

"Yo, Ned." I said. "Most important meal of the day."

"I know. I just want to get this over with, Schaeffer. We've got to find Simon. That damned pot is a curse and I wish I'd never found it."

Our relationship was getting more proximate but not more intimate, as I'd secretly hoped. Still, we were embarking on a journey together, albeit one chaperoned by Veronica Rutherford, the wicked witch of west Santa Fe. I studied Ned's face across the table. It looked weary and sad. His eyelids drooped slightly. His large brown eyes looked tired. Had he not slept?

"We'll find Simon," I said, and smiled my bravest smile. Our eyes met above the vase of light-infused violets.

Ned remembered that he had found a picture of Simon, which he took from his wallet. In it Simon was standing with Dorothea against a low wall. Her arm was around his back and they were laughing. Simon was tall and thin, his dark hair brushed back in a traditional ponytail. He wore a white collared shirt and the traditional bolo tie; I tried to memorize his face. "Dorothea," I said to the picture silently, "I'll find him and keep him safe, I promise."

I'd had a little time to reflect on the most significant bit of information we had so far: the cut on Dorothea's ankle. Now that we thought the Oñate pot was with Simon, I inferred that the cut was either a signature—for someone who hated Indians—or a message of some sort that Acoma Pueblo—where the Indian men were so brutally mutilated—was where we should look for Simon. The more I thought about it, the more I thought that Acoma should be our first stop. I was eager to get started and hoping to leave before Veronica showed up.

"Can we take the picture?" I said, putting it into my tote bag as I spoke. Just then Terry Franchot (that's Fran-SHOW) and Walter Scoggins joined us in the kitchen. "Buon giorno," said Terry in his usual busy and important manner. "What time are we planning to leave?"

"As soon as possible," Ned said, clearing away our dishes. Naturally, Terry and Walter knew all about our trip and they were hovering, clearly anticipating that they would be asked to come along on the finding expedition.

"Where are we going first?" asked Terry brightly. "I'd like to come along, of course."

"*We* are looking for Simon," I said pointedly nodding to Ned, "first in Acoma."

"Ah," said Walter Scoggins, "He's an Acoma Pueblo Indian."

"We know that," I said curtly.

"May I come with you?" Walter asked suddenly. "You know, one of the oldest-living women in North America is at Acoma. She's said to be 104. She was interviewed on her 100th birthday and claimed that her secret was sleeping for two straight days, and then staying awake for two straight days her whole life."

"Would that make her just 50 years old," I asked "since she would miss her birthday every other year?"

"Very clever," said Dr. Scoggins. "But truly, I would like to interview her."

"I'm afraid that's not possible," Ned said. "Veronica Rutherford and Schaeffer are coming, and we hope to bring Simon back with us."

"Hence, a seating problem," I added, just in case Walter didn't get the point. "So sorry."

Walter looked wounded and Terry looked aggrieved at being shut out of this important assignment.

"Got to go," I said brightly, tugging on Ned's sleeve and leading the way. We walked briskly out the front door of the center to the old green Subaru that E.J. had left for us.

Ned and I threw small bags into the trunk and climbed in. "I'll start driving," Ned said. "I know the way out of Santa Fe from here and, believe me, getting in and out of Santa Fe is more than half the battle."

"Okay," I said, strapping myself in and hoping for a quick getaway.

Ned turned to me as he adjusted his seat belt and the rear view mirror, and I got to study his face again to see what made his visage so appealing to me. It was a rather long face, with wide set dark eyes, which I may have mentioned before. His hair was light brown and graying in appropriate places. His cheekbones were high, and his nose and chin were strong. His lower lip was just a little fuller than his upper one. To my eyes he was Cary Grant looking soulful.

As I said, I was hoping for a Le Mans Race start—you know, jump in the car and drive away at top speed—before Veronica could arrive. We couldn't wait for her indefinitely, could we? But just as Ned looked over his shoulder to back up the car, a black limousine zipped up and blocked our way, and Veronica got out in full regalia, a slim fur coat made of some smooth but unfortunate mammal and a large number of his unfortunate little mammal friends.

"It's not yet 7 o'clock," she said to us curtly in greeting, as Ned rolled down the window.

Ned made a show of looking at his watch and finding that it ran fast. "Glad you made it, Veronica" he said without enthusiasm.

"Would you like the front seat?" I chimed in warmly.

"No, thank you," Veronica countered. "I'm quite used to being driven while sitting in the back." She climbed in carefully and managed to insinuate that Ned was now wearing a chauffeur's uniform and cap.

Ned flipped the trunk open and Veronica's real chauffeur neatly deposited two small cases: an overnight and a matching hat box, covered with the interlocking monogram of a designer unknown to me.

Just as Ned was about to pull away, Walter Scoggins came running up. "Oh, good," he said heartily. "There's room for me after all!" And he jumped in with a green knapsack in one hand and a tape recorder trailing a cord in the other.

"Well, Ned," Veronica said, as we began again to back up in the driveway, "I suppose you'll be looking for Simon at Acoma Pueblo."

"Yes, we thought we'd start there," he began.

"I hate visiting those wretched Pueblo reservations," Veronica interrupted. "Sovereign Nations, my artichoke! They're just impoverished public housing projects with everyone over five years old selling his wares. They should be ashamed to put their culture on display as they do for the so-called edification of tourists." She folded her arms crossly and pursed her glossy lips.

"I'll have to disagree with you there, Veronica," I opined. "San Juan Pueblo, where E.J., Ned and I were yesterday, was impressive. The crafts co-op, where artisans do display and sell their work, was exceptional. And the Governor could not have been more considerate when he met with us."

A snort was all that came forth from Veronica in the form of rebuttal. Pronouncement, not reasoned discussion, was her preferred mode of communication. She turned her head and looked determinedly out the window.

We had left the inner core of Santa Fe by now and were driving quickly on Route 25 south towards Albuquerque. Although the Sangre de Cristo Mountains were lovely on the left, the view to the right was, to my East Coast eyes, somewhat stark and barren. The hard frozen ground in the crisp morning light was mostly covered with mud or brown grass only sparsely punctuated with little round bushes that, to my untrained eye, looked as though they might turn into tumbleweed and tumble away at any minute.

The green highway signs with white letters announced the small towns that we were not passing through by staying on the highway, places with alluring names such as Golden and Los Ranchos. The highway also badly bifurcated a number of Pueblo reservations, whose central towns we could not see from the road, although the casino owned by each was nicely accessible from the highway. One scene on the left exemplified the old and the new: San Felipe Casino comprised a small building with a large parking lot and huge floodlights, and just on the edge of the parking lot and the lights was a small cluster of cattle—three adults and three little ones—grazing on what was left of the brown grass and the little brown shrubs.

The travelers were quiet through most of the trip. Ned was trying to make good time, and kept his eyes grimly ahead. Veronica looked stonily out the window, Walter dozed, and I alternated between admiring the landscape and Ned's brown wrists against the steering wheel, modestly on view from his rolled up gray sweater.

When we were nearly at Albuquerque about an hour later, Ned turned onto Route 40 West, which would take us to Acoma Pueblo. As the highway crossed under an underpass, I spied a large sign that read Pueblo Indian Culture Center

"Ned," I said quickly, "Can we make a very short stop at the center? I'd just like a quick look."

Well, Veronica agreed that a rest stop was in order though the "museum" had nothing of value. Veronica walked away, while Walter remained sleeping in the back seat. Time was too short for me to visit the center, but on the right side of the courtyard was a large shining sculpture. It was a bronze circle spiraling outwards from the center, traversed by a horizontal metal rod. It looked very much like one of the symbols inside the Oñate cup. A plaque next to it said that its title was "Winter Solstice." "This sculpture," the sign read, "represents the way the Pueblo Indian's ancestors determined the time of the winter solstice. Ceremonies were then planned, resulting in animal and plant fertility dances or rites."

As I was reading the plaque, Ned came up behind me and put his hand lightly on my shoulder.

"Yes, it's similar to the markings on the vessel," he said, reading my thoughts. "It's quite a common symbol in Pueblo stone carvings and paintings."

"What exactly is a solstice?" I asked, preferring to show my ignorance before Veronica re-emerged.

"A solstice is an astronomical event that happens twice each year, when the tilt of the Earth's axis is most inclined away from the sun—the dead of winter and the longest night of the year—or toward the sun—Midsummer night, the longest day of the year."

"While I'm at it, what's an equinox?"

"They're related. The solstices occur in the winter and summer. The equinoxes also occur twice a year, when the sun is exactly vertical, straight overhead, above the equator. The spring equinox is in March and the fall equinox in September. The day and night are exactly 12 hours each on those dates. Many early cultures told the seasons accurately by these astrological events."

"Are these the sort of symbols that Simon would be looking for to prove his astronomical calculations?"

"That very well might be." Ned replied. "But let's get going," he said abruptly. "Can you go kidnap Veronica?"

Before that became necessary, Veronica marched herself out, freshly beautified, cast a baleful glance at the beautiful winter solstice sculpture, and let herself into the back seat of the green Subaru.

"Why don't I drive for a while, Ned?" I asked, "It's a straight road from here, isn't it?"

Ned shrugged and opened the driver's seat and handed me the keys with a slight bow. "Drive fast and wake me when we get to Acoma Pueblo," he said.

So I drove off westward, and very soon everyone was asleep but me, Ned leaning gracefully against the passenger door, Veronica upright and quiet and Walter snoring heavily in the back seat.

The road west from Albuquerque was very straight and much starker than the landscape nearer Santa Fe. The land was pretty flat with very few trees and the afore mentioned small bushes, sometimes in ones and two, sometimes in clusters. The sky was beginning to look threatening, with gray billowy clouds hanging low. In some places, you could see far off the clouds even lower, dropping sheets of cold rain or sleet on the countryside. The speed limit was 70 and the highway, a main east-west route, was filled with of a number of trucks going even faster than that and passing me at will.

Two small problems began to come into focus. One was the presence of a hard-top, low-rider car that I thought had passed by the center the evening before following us back from Veronica's house. I could make out two people in it, but the windows were rolled up and grimy. It looked like a circa-1965 vehicle, a rusted red with a white stripe on the sides and a white trunk. Now, there were a number of these low-rider cars on the road, a New Mexican equivalent of a teenager's hot rod dream, but this one looked awfully familiar.

Also in my rear-view mirror, I kept seeing a small gray truck with red letters announcing the Albuquerque Tortillas Co., Inc., with a street address in Albuquerque and a red and green chile pepper, with little stick figure arms and legs, bracketing the words. It wasn't really sinister looking, but I kept noticing it. It would pass me like the other trucks, but then

I would catch up with it again. Was it keeping track of us, or just carrying too many tortillas?

After about an hour, I saw a sign for a sharp left announcing Acoma Pueblo, 15 miles. I hooked a left and found myself on a narrow two-lane road, veering off into the horizon. Here the land was really bleak, with clouds lowering even further and rain beginning to spatter the windshield. We crossed railroad tracks—I guess the major east-west commercial train—and things got even sadder. Unlike the San Juan Pueblo with its neat houses and yards leading to the central town square, here we were in miles of deserted landscape.

A few miles down the road was a green sign with white letters, Acoma Pueblo, Sky City, 13 miles. A light, misty cold rain started to fall steadily. We were the only ones on the road. I looked in the rear-view mirror, but neither the low-rider nor the gray tortilla truck seemed to be behind me. Maybe this was the only way in and out of the Pueblo and they could keep an eye on us without the bother of driving the 13 miles of rough road in the rain.

Maybe because I've always hugged the East Coast for dear life, this landscape was beginning to depress me. There were essentially no verticals on the horizon except telephone poles and an occasional sign. But the sky was big and always changing. Its constant presence made the flat landscape dynamic.

And just as I got used to the flatness and the big sky, out of nowhere on the left came a great outcropping of stone, which seemed to have been thrust out of the earth, like a giant stretching his foot up. It was 60 feet high, large as a coliseum, and surprisingly flat on top.

I let out a small gasp at the sight of it and slowed down. Ned, who had been quietly watching me for a while, smiled at me and explained. "It's a butte, spelled 'butte' and pronounced 'beaut'," he said. "I remember the first time I saw one. It seemed impossible, extraordinary."

I lowered the window to take a picture with my small digital camera. "Glad I could experience my first butte with you," I said.

I heard a harumph or a snore—I'm not sure which—from the backseat, but Veronica and Walter still seemed to be asleep.

Ned laughed. "You'll see a lot more of them, too." We came upon two more of different sizes; I noticed more clearly that their sides were striated like a Chinese 1000-layered cake or pictures of the Grand Canyon. Except that on this gray and drizzly day the layers were only gray and tan.

"That's why they call Acoma Pueblo 'Sky City,'" Ned said, explaining the green sign we saw as we entered the Pueblo. "The Acoma Indians built their Pueblo on top of a very large butte. When Oñate's men managed to get near the top, by climbing up the sides, the Acomas threw them off. As you recall, that was only a good short-term strategy."

"I know the story."

"Oñate was actually condemned for this cruelty in Spain when he came back home."

"You know, Ned, the slash across Dorothea's ankle—maybe Dorothea herself did that to point us to Acoma Pueblo. She would have been awfully brave to do that."

"You have a fertile mind," Ned said.

"Do you mean a fertile imagination?"

"Not at all," said Ned with a grim laugh. We had been driving fast down the empty road, flat in all directions, except for these beautiful and, to me, always unexpected protrusions of rock, some small and others that could house a small village.

Suddenly, the road climbed abruptly up to the left, hugging a steep cliff and just as suddenly turned into an overlook onto a deep and vast valley to the right. The overlook had a trailer on it, with a family of tourists looking over the side. Large signs forbade picture taking or even sketching the landscape without a permit which, the signs said, could be purchased at the parking lot and temporary center stop below.

So down we went about three miles further into the valley when the road dead-ended at a small parking lot with a temporary shelter as promised.

It was a sad little affair: a double mobile home office with a plastic restroom to the side. The parking lot was sparsely populated—maybe three vans and a camper. Veronica started to stir as we rolled to a stop.

"What God-forsaken place is this?" Veronica said crankily as her eyes worked their way open.

"It's a parking lot, M'Lady," I said under my breath and Ned smiled.

"We're at the base of Acoma Pueblo," Ned said in a normal voice.

"I don't see any Pueblo," said Veronica nastily. "All I see is a porto-office and a porto-potty, and one is as unattractive as the other."

"I don't think you can see the Pueblo from here," I said. "I read in the guidebook that a bus has to take you up to it. It's not accessible by private car."

"Worse and worse," Veronica said.

"You can wait here if you want," Ned said "I thought you were so keen to find the Oñate vessel."

"I'll come." Veronica said with resignation. "Look, there's the bus," she added, spotting a small school bus pulling into the lot. "Why don't you go in and see about arrangements, Ms. Cornell."

For one short moment, I wondered who Ms. Cornell was. Then I remembered it was me—undercover. Although chafing at her peremptory manner, I dutifully got out and went into the trailer. There was a very grim looking young woman selling off-brand colas and bags of Fritos. Both offerings looked as though they had been sitting on the shelf since the Korean War and lacked something in freshness and appeal.

Another gloomy looking woman was sitting behind the cash register, selling tickets for the bus ride tour up to the Pueblo. I bought four. Signs everywhere warned that no photographs could be taken or sketches made without separately bought permission. I recognized that the Pueblo needed money, but the separate fee for sketching or photos seemed a bit much. This Pueblo, so far, had a really bad feel to it after San Juan.

Armed with tickets and a photographic permission for me only, I called out to Walter, who had also come into the trailer and was fingering some really nasty merchandise in the little store area at the side. We exited the trailer, with Walter commenting on whether climate affected longevity. I was glad that it had stopped raining.

Walter and I headed back to the Subaru and were about five feet away when I caught a glimpse of something that shocked me.

CHAPTER 12

"You know my method. It is founded on the observance of trifles."

—Sherlock Holmes

IT WAS A LITTLE THING REALLY. But it didn't feel little. What I saw was Ned in the back seat with Veronica, their heads together in earnest conversation. As Walter and I came out, Veronica and Ned pulled apart, like lovers caught in an elicit embrace.

Have you ever heard or seen something which causes everything in your consciousness to shift? It's a little like seeing one of those movies with a surprise ending (oh…he's been dead all along…) which forces you to replay the whole film in your mind again, trying to read it with the new information.

I suddenly realized that, while I thought I knew the players and their relationships, it was common pride, nay hubris, which led me to think I could walk into a situation and understand everything. I was like Sophocles' Oedipus, who, just because he had once solved a riddle from a Sphinx, thought he knew everything about everything. And pride, we all know, in addition to being a deadly sin, can lead to marrying a close relative and putting out your own eyes. I was definitely going to do a mid-course correction and not let it go that far.

All right, Ned and Veronica? Intimate in a boudoir sense? Possibly. Both attractive and unattached. Linked together in other ways—but how, why? Were they just after the same bounty? Or were they co-conspirators, even co-criminals? I was not sorry to think of Veronica in this light. She was the classic rich, snobbish, beautiful woman you'd like to have a reason to hate. But Ned, *my Ned,* who looked at me as the light pierced the violets on the table this morning. No, it couldn't be. But everything he did now—like Cary Grant in the Hitchcock movie *Suspicion,* carrying a possibly-poisoned glass of milk up the stairs to his wife—I would have to view with distrust.

Ned and Veronica got out of the car without speaking and took their excursion tickets from me.

Suddenly I started to blather, "You know that you're supposed to stay with the tour guide when we get to the top, and it's a truncated tour, because of the weather, so we can't go into the houses, and we are absolutely forbidden to take pictures or sketch, because I didn't spring for the extra $10 each."

Veronica said, "Then how are we going to find out if Simon is here?"

"Ned," I said, "you make inquiries on the bus and let me know if you learn anything and I'll follow any leads you may have. I'll quietly leave the group while you're enjoying the official tour."

"Don't mind me," Walter said, "but I'm splitting off to find and interview the oldest woman in Acoma, the one who is rumored to be 104."

"Yes, the one who sleeps two days on and two days off like a medical school resident," I said sourly.

"Precisely. I'd like to understand if she has any dietary secrets as well. Or sleeps in a particular position. A Ms. Hongo of Kamato, Japan, claimed her secret to her 116 years was a daily snack of unrefined brown sugar and a glass of sake."

"All right," I said. "I guess they're used to crazy tourists."

We all mounted a minivan with a taciturn driver and a very surly guide. Was this the Acoma mind set? People at San Juan Pueblo had been so friendly and helpful. These people seemed angry about something, possibly Oñate and the feet cut off. I wondered if I would be able to let that go either, even though it was about 400 years before.

There were about 14 of us in the minivan: an Australian family of four who looked bouncy in khakis and windbreakers, and who all had cameras and photo permission cards around their necks. There was an elderly couple probably traveling in the RV in the parking lot, and an American family with three teenagers, who looked embarrassed to be seen with their parents even in this desolate outpost of civilization where they were extremely unlikely to see anyone they knew from school. They looked blank and stayed connected to their earphones.

The guide, Dolores, welcomed us in a monotone patter, which came out as if it were one long word: "I'myourguidecallmeDolores." She continued to talk in this way as the minivan wound its way up the very steep mesa, about 400 feet high. For most of its existence, I think she said, there was no paved road up the mountain until 1952 when Hollywood producers wanted to use Acoma Pueblo as a movie set.

Of course, this 400-foot high plateau was terrific in defending against enemy attacks, but really bad for collecting staples, which they had to haul up in a laborious process. Now, Dolores said balefully, only about 50 Acomas lived on top of the mesa year round but many more came for festivals and holidays.

We bumped and spun our wheels up and up the mesa side until we lurched to a halt in a concrete road, pitted with potholes. The light rain had starting falling again, collecting in the watery clay cavities.

Veronica, who was sitting in the first seat of the van, got out and deposited one of her very expensive lizard-skin decoratively stitched boots into the muck. With one clean movement, she walked a few paces, turned around and climbed right back in the bus.

"You'll find me here," she said curtly, looking at Ned, "when you finish your tour."

As the group assembled against a rock and old adobe wall, I turned quickly to Ned, "Any advice on finding Simon?"

"The van driver said that his mother's house is left from the church, the third door down."

"Thanks, Ned. I'll slip away quietly."

"As will I," said Walter in a stage whisper, his Van Dyke beard bobbing in an unbecoming manner.

Dolores then lined us all up against a nasty adobe wall as though we were going to be shot, but instead of asking us if we required a blindfold, she continued her guide patter in her guide monotone:

"As I said on the bus, because of the weather we are only going to have a half-tour and cannot visit the houses of the Acoma Pueblo but only the church." There was a little glimmer of joy in her tour-guide voice as she repeated this bad news to us. "Acoma Pueblo," she continued, "is known for its exceptionally thin-walled pottery, decorated with complex black geometric designs carefully painted on a white background... ."

I was beginning to think she meant to keep us out in the rain permanently, but finally she said without emphasis, "Follow me now to the famous church of San Esteban del Rey Mission."

In sad single file, Ned, Walter and I padded in the row of tourists. Walter veered off left when we turned right. Veronica, I believe, remained in the van—at least I thought I saw her proud head erect in silhouette as we rounded the corner. As I looked back, I was also alarmed to see the red low-rider pull up and park a few spaces behind the minivan with Veronica in it. I was about to break off and make enquiries—and now check out the familiar low-rider—when Dolores doubled back and rounded us up like dogies on a cattle drive and directed us up to the steps of the Mission church. The site was, in fact, astounding. The church overlooked the side of the mesa and a church yard with an incredibly steep drop. From the outside, it was a beautifully proportioned grand mission church, its majesty somewhat mitigated by the knowledge, which Dolores was keen to supply, that it was built on the backs of Acoma slave labor, but later embraced as the Acoma combined their native faith with Catholicism. Wooden planks had been put down in front of the grand facade so that we could climb the crumbling front steps to the massive front door.

As we turned our back to the facade, we could see a Native graveyard, surrounded by low walls and extending to the edge of the mesa. The view, even in the mist and drizzle, was awe-inspiring. The height and isolation of the place was intense. The gray walls around the churchyard were about waist high and were capped with fearsome gargoyle-like heads apparently meant to keep evil spirits and everyone else away. It seemed to be working. Nothing was in sight but a lone chicken scratching forlornly in the dirt.

I was getting impatient to break away and check things out, when Dolores entered the church and everyone followed in a line. I peeked into the church, a handsome lofty structure, painted in bright colors, including pink for the confessionals. Dolores was saying something about the Acoma women painting the interior every year with Catholic symbols as well as native motifs of the sun, moon, stars, as well as ears of corn—when I doubled back, sneaked out the front door of the church, walked swiftly down the wooden planks, out the church yard, and into the street of the Pueblo. A brief glance to my left indicated that the red low-rider was there and apparently abandoned, and that Veronica was either not in the minivan or slumped in her seat.

I proceeded straight down the narrow and deserted Pueblo street, all made of stone and adobe. Following Ned's directions, I picked my way to the third adobe house on the left and knocked timidly on the door. This was meant to be Simon's mother's house.

There was no answer to my knock so I turned the handle of the door and went in. It looked empty. It was one room of stone, cold and bare. It had an adobe cooking stove or *horno*, I think they're called, in the corner, but no fire. There was no electricity or discernable plumbing. A ceramic water jar and basin stood on a low table; there was also a single bed and a wooden bookcase, crammed with books and papers.

"Simon," I called out, suddenly frightened of the silence. "Simon," I tried again just in case I'd missed a hiding place.

No, the place was deserted. But—oh my goodness, on the floor was a set of muddy footprints, coming in near mine, walking around the room and then, I thought, leaving again. I touched the nearest print, and was struck to see that—although not watery, the clay/mud mixture was still moldable and retained some moisture. This had to be a newish print, probably from today. I examined the prints. They were from the ubiquitous cowboy boots, fairly large—maybe size 12 men's. Not a woman's surely. Were these Simon's prints? Or someone else's?

I quickly searched the quadrants of the room. The bookshelf, which had first caught my attention, had books and notebooks all about archaeo-astronomy—Simon's study and passion. The notebooks were in careful order and I took the last one. I could always give it back. Behind a black curtain, there was another small cot and some pitiful clothes. There was also a pair of moccasins—the kind that wrap around the ankles and legs and are used in ritual dancing. I held one up and compared the size to the muddy print. The moccasin was smaller by several sizes. So the footprint wasn't Simon's.

The last thing I looked at was a small carved box, which contained ceramic fragments, and some of them had petroglyphs in them; one was a spiral, like the one I had seen on the wall of the Pueblo Center in Albuquerque, representing the winter stolstice.

A sharp noise at the door of Simon's house made me start and jerk my head around. The wooden door let light in only around the edges and I could see nothing outside.

I dropped the shards of ceramic back into the box and made quickly for the door. To my dismay, I found that it was locked shut from the outside.

For heaven's sake, I thought to myself, who is chasing whom here? I'm just minding my own business, doing some quiet and harmless snooping, and someone wants me to stop. Talk about an unhealthful work environment, I thought indignantly.

I looked around the room for a way to get out or a means of getting the door open. Now that I knew that I was stuck, my easily aroused claustrophobia was beginning to rear its head.

Taking several deep, cleansing breaths trying to calm myself, I looked around the room for an implement and found in the corner, an axe.

Wielding an axe at a locked door was not my usual mode of making an exit. Axe-wielding was not really in my repertoire. Even wielding the big hammer at the Virginia Renaissance Fair had resulted in my not even coming close to ringing the bell, but actually ending up in the category of "Plague Victim."

Nonetheless, I shouldered the axe and made a good faith swing at the door near the doorknob. Five or six of these efforts yielded success and I was able to step through the doorframe. I can tell you that I was glad to see that drizzly, low hanging sky. I went back for Simon's notebook, the shards of pottery and started back out the door.

But I stopped short and shifted a scream. The barrel of a gun was suddenly against my chest and I could feel its heavy metal weight against me.

CHAPTER 13

"I've often wondered how these murderous fellows manage to keep in shape while they're contemplating their next effort."

—*P.G. Woodhouse,* Carry on, Jeeves

AT THE OTHER END OF THE GUN was a really scary guy. He looked like he was a linebacker from Georgia Tech, who had been sidelined for rough behavior. He had a broad face, creamy dark skin and wavy black hair. His face was wide and fat, and his dark eyes consequently looked squinty. The parts of his thick forearms that were visible were covered with miscellaneous black tattoos. He was wearing jeans, boots and a black sweatshirt embossed with a skull and the words, "Mother, May I Kill Today?" This I took to be a very bad sign. Across a dinner table with friends, I would no doubt have admired his Gothic flair and wanted to know all about him. Across the barrel of a gun, I was less enthused.

"Who are you?" I said, trying to make my voice authoritative and indignant. Instead my voice came out a combination of Breathy and Squeaky, two of Snow White's lesser-known dwarfs.

"Who wants to know?" was his witty answer.

We stared at each other for a long moment.

"You find what you were looking for?" He said, staring at my pocket book.

"No. Did you?" I couldn't believe that we were acting like playground bullies, standing in the cold rain, outside Sky City, Acoma Pueblo, one of us holding a weapon.

Suddenly, a large meaty hand shot out and grabbed my purse, turning it upside down so that everything fell out on the ground: lipstick, camera, flashlight, iPhone, pens, Simon's last notebook and the pottery shard with the solstice sign.

We both looked down at the soggy mess. Bubba, as I dubbed the linebacker in my mind, looked disappointed that I didn't have what he was looking for. Could it have been Oñate's drinking vessel? At least this particular opponent hadn't found it yet either.

"I don't know what you were looking for, but I clearly don't have it," I said, and knelt down to salvage the items on the ground. As I knelt I came face to face with Bubba's cowboy boots, about a size 12, I'd say. So those boots probably made the footprints inside Simon's house. I guessed he had searched the house just as I had and hadn't found Oñate's drinking cup either. That was a relief because I wouldn't have known how to get it back from him.

I got up slowly making no sudden moves. We were back to the staring contest.

"Stay out of my business," he said to me. "This is your warning." He pushed the barrel of the gun more forcefully against me. My standard witty repartee deserted me as I felt the metal gun barrel again, hard against my ribs.

"Who sent you?" I gasped out, hoping to find in this information the silver lining to this unfortunate encounter.

Bubba just laughed, which came out like a snarl.

"I'm not foolin' with you," he said. His left hand came at my shoulder and hit me with enough force to send me back against the adobe wall of Simon's house and, before I knew it, I was sitting winded on muddy ground. Bubba gave my belongings a mean kick with his hard heel boot, splashing the sludge up at my face, and walked quickly away.

I found a dry tissue, mopped my face and put my belongings back in my handbag, feeling glad that I had an old ratty one and had not indulged in a the beaded leather Santa Fe one that E.J. had urged me to buy. As I stood up, I realized that I was cold, stiff, minimally bruised and out of breath. Bubba's light-touch warning had packed a wallop, and I was glad to see him gone. Why people recommend keeping your enemies close, I really couldn't imagine. And who had sent the self-styled Terminator anyway? It never occurred to me that he was flying solo. He had "henchman" written all over him. Someone—maybe several people—really wanted Oñate's cup and were trying to find Simon to get it.

So I was getting myself together to meet the others back at the beautiful San Esteban del Rey Mission church when—from the direction of the church came a blood-curdling scream.

CHAPTER 14

**"Opening a bus window in N.Y.
with the left hand in front of
Bellevue you might get a
hernia.
Walking across First Avenue
you might stumble into a
pothole
& get your head run over by a
taxicab."**

—*Allen Ginsberg, "You Might Get In Trouble"*

IT SOUNDED LIKE A MAN'S SCREAM, and it had a falling-away sound, like when Wylie E. Coyote falls off the cliff into the Grand Canyon, leaving a coyote-shaped crater on the ground. That's not really so far-fetched an image when you're in Sky City, Acoma, on a mesa 400 feet above the canyon below.

I swallowed hard and ran toward the sound in time to see the assorted tour group members all leaning over the cemetery wall at the front of the church and looking down with horror.

"What happened?" I said, as I grabbed Ned from behind and turned him around. "What is it?" It's the sort of question you ask, kind of not wanting to know the answer.

"It's Walter," said Ned, his voice tight, his face ashen.

Veronica stood next to him and swayed as if she were ready to faint.

I pushed between them and looked over. There was nothing to see but sheer crumbly rock face with a few plants hanging on, only weakly determined to take root.

"My God," I said. "How do you know it's Walter? Did anyone see this?"

"I don't know. It all happened so fast. We heard a scream that sounded like Walter and rushed over. Here's his notebook next to the wall," Ned said.

"Not good," I said grimly. "This cemetery wall is too high for a grown man to fall off of. He had to have been pushed. We've got to go find him. He might be alive down there."

By this time, a member of the Acoma Pueblo police had come up to investigate the situation. He was slight and middle-aged, but strong and wiry, wearing his gun belt low on his torso. He had on what we call a cowboy hat (should these be called cowboy and Indian hats?) and a large silver badge.

Just as he was about to question us, we all froze in place as we heard a faint, disembodied voice coming from about thirty feet below. "Help me, help me," it sang up sadly.

We all looked at each other. Actually, Veronica looked at Ned, I looked at Veronica, and Ned looked at me.

"Ned will go," Veronica said, "Won't you?"

"Of course," Ned said.

"Wait," I said, not wanting to think it, but fearing that if Ned had pushed him in the first place, this could be an opportunity to finish him off. "I'm good at this."

"At what?" Veronica snapped, "Jumping off chasms and rescuing men twice your size? Ridiculous."

While we jockeyed for the questionable opportunity to risk our lives on a rope off a sheer cliff, the Acoma policeman had secured a sturdy rope ladder to an iron post, had thrown it over the side, and was making his way down with considerable skill, rappelling off the cliff, toward Walter's sad, desperate voice.

Ten minutes later, we saw Walter coming slowly up the rope ladder followed by the policeman, who was pushing him up from below. Walter managed a weak smile as we took his arms and pulled him the rest of the way up. Walter planted his feet on safe ground and shook himself off.

"Your friend was very lucky," said the Acoma policeman. "His tape recorder extension cord caught on a tree stub, and held him till I got there. He'll live to be 100."

"I certainly hope so," said Walter, who was bruised and shaken. "I've researched it enough."

"Yes," said the policeman, allowing himself a smile. "He's charmed. He'll outlive us all."

He turned back to his Acoma friends and talked to them in a Tewa language.

"Walter, are you all right? What happened?" I asked.

"I'm all right," Walter said weakly. "But not really. Somebody pushed me off that cliff. Somebody wants me dead." He looked with fear at me, Ned, and Veronica. "I'll tell you about it later. I want to get out of here."

The bus was already loaded by the time we got back. Unexpectedly, Dolores, the tour guide, showed a few signs of life on the way down. Here was a story for tour leaders to incorporate into their patter for years to come. Maybe the story would be about the stupidity of tourists. Maybe it would become folklore, like the spirits of the Acoma Indians getting back at the Anglos. Many possibilities.

At the bottom of the mesa, we got off the bus and into our car, Ned driving again and Veronica next to him. As we headed back to the highway, I noticed that the red low-rider, no doubt graced with Bubba and his teammates, had already left. We needed to find Simon, at least before Bubba did, and I needed to find out who wanted Walter dead.

The Navajos, I remembered from Dolores's comments, fear death, and purify and exorcize anyone or anything that comes in contact with it. The Pueblo Indians, on the other hand, embrace death as part of life, perhaps under the influence of Mexican immigrants, who welcome spirits back on All Souls' Day with wine and feasting at the cemetery. I guess I was part Navajo. I didn't like death one bit.

CHAPTER 15

"God writes a lot of comedy—the trouble is he's stuck with bad actors that don't know how to play funny."

—Garrison Keillor

WALTER SAID HE NEEDED A STIFF DRINK although the rest of us wanted to keep going. Without other guidance, we planned to head west on Route 40, which parallels the old Route 66, to Gallup, where we knew that Philip had a part-time job and probably another pied à terre, which I hoped was less humble and more convenient than the one at Acoma. Gallup was a good launching spot for expeditions into Chaco Canyon.

"Why don't you drink what's in your thermos," Veronica said tartly, referring to an aggressively Earth-friendly green glass thermos attached to Walter's belt loop.

"You're right," Walter said. "I always carry 'Maya Elixir' from the Longevity Café in Santa Fe."

I enquired about the Longevity Café to distract Walter and help him recover his serenity. Apparently, it was a full-service longevity center, which combined herbal and physical remedies for reversing the aging process. Walter swore by the Maya Elixir, which was certified to increase life span considerably. Walter took out some paper cups, gulped a dose down with a satisfied sigh and offered me a taste, which I accepted. I could use a little longevity insurance, I thought.

The drink, still warm from the thermos, was a spicy blended drink of indescribable flavors, sort of like Mary Poppins' medicine that tasted simultaneously of buttered toast and cherry tart. Unfortunately, the flavors in the Maya Elixir were more like calf's liver and onions mingling with a rancid pot of tea. I had no doubt that longevity or even eternal life would be mine for the drinking, except that I expected to be dead by the time I finished it.

"Thanks," I sputtered. "Do you have anything to go with it?" I needed to get that taste out of my mouth.

Walter happily passed me some Longevity Café patented trail mix in a large plastic bag, also embossed with the name of its origin. Trail mix or GORP, as we used to call it, Good Old Raisin and Peanuts, is high on energy, composed of sweet, salty and oily things. Walter's trail mix, on the other hand, was no fun at all, consisting mainly of dry, tasteless seeds of several varieties. The age-old query, "Is it a long life or does it just seem long?" took on new meaning.

"Thanks, Walter," I said trying to clear my throat. At least the Maya Elixir taste was somewhat diluted.

"I'm sorry, everyone," said Walter suddenly. "I still need a drink."

"Okay, okay," I said, and Ned took a sharp left off the highway to get to a casino on the other side of the roadway, called "Sky City Casino," clearly owned by the Acoma and standing on its sovereign land. We pulled up into the parking lot, which was pretty empty, it being about 4 o'clock. There were no low-riders that I could see—just a few late-model American cars and a red pick-up filled with hay and two sad-looking dogs, a little rodent-faced mongrel and an irritated-looking German Shepherd chained on top.

Inside the casino, it was clean and well-lighted with a large gas fire in a hearth in the lobby. In front of us were the slot machines in a dimly-lighted room, making clicks, whirs, and buzzes, and the occasional rattle of nickels being sent out of the slot and into plastic cups held by the patrons to catch windfalls.

I took a seat on the warm ledge of the hearth while Veronica and Ned went into the coffee and gift shop. As soon as they were gone, Walter sat down next to me and grasped my sleeve.

"It had to be one of them who pushed me," he said furtively.

"Why would they do that?" I asked.

"Because I saw them plotting with one another in the back seat this morning. They don't want me to know what they're up to."

"But what are they up to?"

"I don't know," Walter said dejectedly.

"Then it's not likely that they need you out of the way," I said. After a minute I asked, "By the way, did you see any formidable bodyguard types near you?"

Walter shook his head. "You know, Ned used to work for Veronica," he said thoughtfully, "acquiring some of her collections for her. Maybe they're after the Oñate vessel for their own reasons."

"No doubt they are," I murmured, tucking this piece of information away. Ned was in a dependent relationship with Veronica; how far did this go? Was he also her boy-toy?

Walter just sat glumly. "I'm afraid to be alone now. I can hardly live to be a centenarian if I'm cut down in my prime by this trip."

"I'll try to keep an eye on you, Walter," I said. "Your research is one of my top priorities," I added wondering if comprehending irony was within his range.

A cocktail waitress in a French-maid, but very respectable, knee-length skirt, came by with cherry colored soft drinks in plastic cups. Walter declined his sadly. "Can't even get a decent drink in here," he said, "whereas in France, where many of the super-centenarians live, a glass of red wine is always available." Walter excused himself and went into the coffee shop.

I sat on the hearth as people drifted in and out. Everyone was Indian but me, and although some English was spoken, I truly felt as though I were in a foreign country. Well, we were, after all, in the sovereign nation of Acoma Pueblo.

It was easy enough to strike up a conversation and to make enquiries about Acoma residents and I immediately realized that I had struck gold as to my enquiries on Simon.

I got to talking to one tall, thin older man who had very nice teeth, which, I realized only belatedly, were too nice to be real. He was Acoma and knew Simon, but hadn't seen him in a while. My God, this was a small world and good for investigations. I met a friendly, middle-aged woman, who was a potter and sold her signature pots at Acoma Pueblo on nice days, black and white ceramic vases with wide necks. She had learned pottery from her mother, and now had four daughters, two of whom worked in the casino. One was a "miracle baby," she told me, who was born weighing only one pound. I assumed that she had named her miracle baby something appropriate like "Milagros," which is 'miracle' in Spanish, but she told me she had called her "Wilma." I sighed. Is a sense of wonder really dead? But the potter did know Simon, who was a distant relative on her mother's side. She said that he was always thought of as the "crazy genius" in the family. Simon, she said, had left the Acoma reservation and had gone to school to study archaeology at the University of Arizona... or was it California? He had been a dreamy kid, but when he came back, he had a new passion, to find out where the Acoma had come from, and whether they were direct descendants of the ancient people who deserted Chaco Canyon suddenly and left monuments to a huge civilization in the desert, not too far from here. He spent his time mostly out in the desert looking for evidence. When he wasn't there or at Acoma, he was in Gallup, where he had a job selling Indian jewelry at Richardson's, a store there. And hadn't he married a San Juan Pueblo woman a few years back? Simon, she told me, was handsome, mysterious, and attractive. It was a disappointment to his family when he didn't amount to anything.

I was more grateful than I could say to the Acoma potter, who had told me more about Simon than I would ever have learned otherwise. I offered to come back on a clear day to buy one of her pots, but hoped secretly that this would be my one and only visit.

So I had a picture of Simon now: a dreamer, a scholar, a man obsessed with the desert and its remains as clues to the secrets of the Pueblos. And at the center of his quest was ancient Chaco Canyon. I'd have to read up about that in my guidebook, and how it might be connected to the infamous Oñate vessel.

I had said goodbye to my new acquaintance and met up with Ned and Veronica, who wanted to drive on to Gallup right away, but Walter insisted on finding a real drink and a place to spend the night. I suggested leaving Walter behind, but he was much too terrified. Finally, Veronica gave in and Ned agreed. When we got to the car, I got out my trusty guide to New Mexico and noted a bed and breakfast, about 20 miles west and on our way to Gallup. It was called "Cibola," which Ned said was a mythical city of gold, which the Spaniards had hoped to find near here in New Mexico, just as they had found the Aztec's cities of gold in Mexico City.

Of course, Ned said, they'd never found gold here. They found the Ancient Pueblo civilization called Anasazi at Chaco Canyon, which was architecturally rich, but turquoise, not gold, was its major precious item. I thought that turquoise was more beautiful than gold, but clearly the conquistadors didn't agree with me. Perhaps that's why they were all the more vicious when they couldn't find it.

We turned North off Route 40 west and toward signs for Chaco Canyon, which was about 90 minutes further north and then into the small town of Grants, through which a railroad track ran its full length. There we saw a small sign for Cibola. I used my iPhone, which got a signal about 20% of the time here in New Mexico, to call ahead and make a reservation for four.

We followed a dirt road for about a mile, the land mostly fenced in with horses, cows and llamas roaming quietly and eating the meager grass in the darkening mist. In about a mile we came to an another improbable sight: Cibola B&B was surrounded by the walls of a full-fledged Spanish hacienda, the sort of place where Zorro climbed up the trellises, vanquished señoritas, and made the sign of the Z.

Just a half hour ago we had been in Indian country, at the top of the cliff where Spaniards had been thrown down. Now we were suddenly in the Spanish colonial past. As if my mind were not already in an anthropological swirl, our Cibola bed-and-breakfast hosts came running out to greet us as we pulled up, looking like '60s-era, middle-aged hippies.

Veronica got out of the car and looked disdainfully at the owners of the hacienda, obviously finding them the unworthy heirs of a noble tradition. Ned came forward though and shook their hands, eliciting a small snort from Veronica. We each took our small bags with us, Veronica waiting till Ned took up hers as well, and followed our hosts, who turned out to be River and Brook Orkins from Los Angeles, former entertainment lawyers, they told us immediately, who had chucked everything to live a Simpler Life. Let me just say, for the record, that the signs of stress of a Simpler Life were already showing through a thin veneer. Brook's long brown braided hair needed a wash, and River's bell-bottom cuffs were frayed.

Bed and Breakfasts, or B&Bs, are a strange sub-species of hotel. They're small and intimate, and the owners see themselves somewhere between hoteliers and old family friends. River and Brook welcomed us like the latter, and were pathetically eager to see us. The bad weather, they told us, though no one had asked, had made for a slow season, and all four hacienda rooms at Cibola were available. Would we like to see them?

"I need a drink," said Walter in a monotone. It was instructive to see that in a real crisis Walter turned to alcohol rather than to Maya Elixir to calm his nerves.

"What were we thinking?" said Brook to River. "River, could you get some wine and glasses? I'll bring in a few hors d'oeuvres that I whipped up."

Brook and River disappeared out separate doors, and left us standing in a little front room filled with atmospheric icons of old Spain as well as a modern-day credit card machine.

"We're leaving at 6 a.m. tomorrow," hissed Veronica when we were alone. "I can't believe I'm staying here with you in this God forsaken place with a would-be killer on the loose."

"It's okay, Veronica," Ned said wryly. "The killer, whoever he is, doesn't seem to be after you."

In an instant, River and Brook appeared from separate doors and guided us out of the front room to a beautiful little inner courtyard, surrounded on all sides with the rooms of the hacienda. Frankly, with its high walls, the Cibola hacienda looked plenty fortified against intruders, including conquistadors. The possible dangers within were another matter.

Even Veronica murmured in surprise at how lovely the courtyard was. Strands of white lights hung from the walls and small fruit trees, and garlanded the well in the center of the courtyard. Candles in white paper bags—called farolitos here—outlined the square of the courtyard and the paths leading to the central well. A lovely wood fire in a copper basin gave off heat and light next to a wooden table near the closest inner wall, and it was set with wine glasses, bottles of red and white wine, and a plate full of warm canapés and little ham sandwiches on French bread.

Walter went directly for the red wine—conducive to longevity, as he pointed out, and we all had lovely California Napa Valley wine, and spinach and cheese in perfect puff pastries. We gasped with pleasure and delight, and made appreciative murmuring noises for the next few minutes.

Our hosts were happy that we were happy and, hungry for conversation, told us all about how they had been successful lawyers in L.A. representing Reba McEntire and Gloria Estefan, but had come to New Mexico on vacation and fallen in love with this old hacienda from the 17th century and had been fixing it up room by room. Unfortunately, business had been slow, and River's memoirs about the life of an L.A. entertainment lawyer were going slowly, too.

Veronica soon got bored with these stories, and having eaten and drunk sufficiently, she brusquely asked River and Brook to show us to our rooms. The layout of rooms was linear around the courtyard, each leading into the next, around the square. The first room belonged to our hosts, the next, Veronica claimed, as the safest, and she demanded that Ned protect her other flank with the next adjoining room. Not wanting to be next to Ned or Veronica, Walter selected the last room backing up to the living room where we first came in, so I took the buffer room in between Ned's and Walter's. The rooms were all furnished within an inch of their lives with authentic and very dressy period furnishings featuring woven hangings, tapestries, stuffed chairs and formidable wood armoires. Each tiny room was identified by its predominant color: gold, blue, red, and green (mine was the red room). Each had a cute little wood stove, which came with two laminated pages of instructions, beginning with the cautionary words in large black italics of what to do "If the Fire Has Spread to the Rug." I decided to forgo a fire that night and hoped the others would as well.

Alone now, I didn't really feel secure enough to take off my clothes. I decided to practice my T'ai Chi form, which I had neglected for several days and would no doubt pay the price with a sub-par Fist Under Elbow and Ride the Tiger. After about 20 minutes of practice followed by quiet breathing, I completed the form and thought that, even though Master Zhang would probably have swatted me several times with a rolled-up newspaper, I felt stronger and more relaxed. I was ready to sleep, and got into the very cozy soft bed, its mattress's sleep number about minus five. I was fully dressed except for my shoes and hoped that I could fall asleep quickly, since Ned had already paid up and asked our hosts to wake us at 5:30 a.m. for a 6 a.m. departure.

I had turned off my light, and could see a little as my eyes got accustomed to the dark outside my curtained window to the courtyard. I was thinking over today's events, and feeling reasonably safe for the night. No car had followed us to the hacienda that I had seen. And yet, one of my own team members might be a killer or would-be killer. Ned was clearly troubled, even haunted, and was keeping secrets that had to do with Veronica. Veronica wouldn't hesitate to walk with her fancy lizard boots over her own grandmother. Walter was flakey, obsessive and self-absorbed, but could this be an elaborate act? And could he have thrown himself over the cliff to divert suspicion from himself?

Someone—perhaps a few doors from mine—had killed the Indian docent Dorothea, Simon's wife... and who had sent Bubba to rough me up? It could have been any one of my traveling companions. With these thoughts, I became more alert and was glad that I'd stayed in my clothes ready for fight or flight. Soon, in the quiet of the silent hacienda, I began to hear sounds—it was hard to tell if they were in the middle distance or nearer. Were they coyotes? Llamas? Do llamas make sounds? The door on the armoire was creaking open and shut, either from a draft or of its own accord... And just as I was getting seriously creeped out, a door-knob in my room turned quietly.

CHAPTER 16

"I was of three minds, like a tree in which there are three blackbirds."

—Wallace Stevens, "Thirteen Ways of Looking at a Blackbird"

I FROZE IN MY BED, momentarily incapable of action. Then I remembered my deep cleansing breaths and took two very quietly.

The door opened slowly, but it wasn't from the room on either side. It was a door from the courtyard, which I had foolishly thought was a window. Well, that narrowed the identity of the intruder down to approximately everybody. The figure came in slowly and I could discern a reasonably large shadow blocking out the ambient light of the faralitos in the courtyard. Was it large enough for a Bubba? Hard to tell.

The figure went quietly over to my personal items in the overstuffed red leather chair and selected my pocketbook; then it took out a small object—my wallet. So far this intruder seemed more intent on seeking my money rather than my life, and I relaxed and started to plan—although in truth, the wallet check might be preparation to take my money and then my life.

I very gradually moved my feet to the edge of my bed, and down on the ornate heavy Navajo rug on the hardwood floor. Very slowly I maneuvered myself behind the figure and took out my new weapon: a martial arts move called Fair Lady Works the Shuttles. Despite its poetic name, this move entails a vicious forward punch and a severe hatchet chop to the artery on the left side of the neck.

To my surprise, the figure did not crumble to the floor, but rather grabbed my hatchet hand and whirled me around. I guess I needed to work a few more Shuttles before using that move on the job.

A rough voice snarled at me holding my wrist in an unpleasantly tight way. "Who are you?"

It was Ned. I wouldn't have thought him capable of such force or nastiness.

I sputtered back, also in a whisper, "Who are *you*? And why are you in my room going through my things?"

We stood staring at each other in the dark breathing heavily. He studied my face in the dim light as if stealing my secrets. I felt his breath, his body heat, and the energy in his elegant body.

Gradually, Ned relaxed his grip on my hand, but kept his hold on my wrist in case I were getting ready to bolt.

"All right," he said, more calmly, "I don't believe you are who you say you are—an old college friend of E.J.'s, the niece of Joseph Cornell. It doesn't wash."

"So who do you think I am?" I said, wondering why I was on the defensive, with an intruder in my own room where I was, for once, quietly, if temporarily, minding my own business.

"I think you're an FBI agent, if you must know, and I was looking to find out for sure."

"And why would you care?" I countered. "Are the FBI agents after you?" .

"Actually, yes." The silence fell again while I took this in.

"Is this a long story? Because my hand is getting bruised and my feet are getting cold."

Ned relaxed gradually into the gentler Ned I was used to, apologized, and suggested we go out to the courtyard so as not to wake the others. He released my wrist and stepped carefully outside. I slipped on my shoes, my jacket, and grabbed a large quilt comforter. When I emerged, Ned had poured two glasses of red wine left from our late supper and had found a small sofa rocker for two. I offered half the comforter and we sat on the opposite sides and looked hard at each other. Were we adversaries or friends? The connection was still there for me, as when we had looked at each other over the sunlit vase of violets at breakfast that morning, but I was now on my guard. Was he using the old Cary Grant charm on me deliberately to throw me off his very attractive scent? I stared further. Some people strike me as so beautiful that I'm almost afraid to look at them carefully. There was a faded beauty in Ned's face, but also a shadow of something. Pain? Fear? Obsession?

"I'm listening," I said quietly.

"This is hard for me to tell you," He paused. "Some years ago, when you were just a child"— I couldn't help smiling at that—"I had just finished my Doctoral dissertation on pre-Colombian pottery, and I was rather badly in debt. On one of my research trips to New Mexico, I met Veronica M. Rutherford, who was then an even more stunning woman and a voracious collector." He paused, wondering how to continue.

"Go on," I urged quietly.

"As you probably know, there has always been a huge black market in Indian artifacts, with choice pieces from public or Reservation sites somehow getting to collectors when they should be retained for the public or Indian use. I'm ashamed to say that Veronica, using methods that appealed to several of my baser instincts, persuaded me to obtain one such artifact for her. I did it only once, and I've always regretted it."

"Does anyone else know this?"

"No. It's between me and Veronica…and now you. But it's coming back to haunt me. Now Veronica wants the Oñate vessel very badly and she's threatened to let my secret out unless I help her get it."

I thought about this, and noted that Veronica was just as nasty as she seemed. "What would happen if you just publicly confessed?"

"Well, the statue of limitations had run out a long time ago on the offense. But my reputation and the confidence that people—like E.J.—have in me would be ruined. I don't think I'd get to work again in my field. I couldn't stand that."

"So if the Oñate vessel came your way?"

"I really don't know what I'd do. I guess I'm hoping that someone else finds it first."

"Oh, Ned." I couldn't help feeling sorry for him. "If it's any comfort, I'll certainly try to find it first. But Veronica... she'll always have this hold over you. There's no telling what she'll ask you to do next."

"I've thought of that."

"I suppose you have." We sipped our wine quietly. That night had turned clear and cold. A half moon shone above the starry sky, large and bright.

"It's your turn," Ned said finally.

"My turn?" I asked.

"What are you doing here and are you an FBI agent?"

"If I were, you'd be in big trouble," I laughed. Ned didn't. "Really, I'm here for E.J., to help and support her. She called me and told me of the problem at the center. She just wants the Oñate vessel restored before the Board of Trustees ousts her from the best job she ever had."

"Are you really an artist?"

"Isn't everyone in Santa Fe? My great uncle, Joseph Cornell invented the art form of the box within the box. What's inside often contradicts what's outside, don't you think?"

"Not always," Ned said defensively. "So you're not an FBI agent?"

I shrugged. "You wouldn't believe me either way. And you certainly wouldn't find any proof in my wallet."

Ned was quiet for a moment. "Schaeffer," he turned to me and moved closer, "if we both…if we all get through this, I'd like…" he stopped.

I turned toward him and dared to look at him carefully. He was very handsome, earnest and sad.

"I'd like that, too," I murmured, not really knowing what I had agreed to. Ned moved closer and put his arm around me gently. Then he reached up and put his hand under my chin, tilting my face toward his. When his lips touched mine, I knew I was in a Cary Grant and Ingrid Bergman movie. His lips were soft, his kiss long, sweet, and tentative. I imbibed his warmth and his pain. My right hand went up to touch his chest. Its warmth surprised me and I wanted to keep my hand there and gather it in. I rested my head against his shirt. It felt good to rest there, his hands behind my back holding me still, his chin resting in my hair.

Finally, gathering my wits about me, I pulled back. Cary Grant is sometimes the murderer, I reminded myself. I gave an exasperated shiver, and sat back against Ned's encircling arm. "Thank you for telling me all this, Ned," I said. "May this story have a happy ending."

Ned walked me to my door, kissed me once more, and I went in and locked the door carefully behind me. These haciendas, for all their high walls, were not so very secure after all. And my defenses? I rated myself B+ for Information Gathering and F for Level Head on Shoulders. Perhaps, after all, I should check out Ned's story with Veronica.

 மமம

River and Brook came around in the courtyard at 5:30 a.m. as requested, ringing the kind of bells that call Tibetan monks to prayer. In truth, it was a lovely way to wake up, if not very effective. There's nothing like a horrible buzzing sound next to one's head that won't turn off to get one going in the morning. But the bells eventually had their desired effect, and we all emerged in different states of wakefulness into the courtyard. From there, River and Brook led us into a kitchen, with a table big enough for six. It was a lovely old wood table, dressed with beautiful glazed clay dishes in a pumpkin color, and huge ceramic coffee mugs by each plate. I noted that each place and mug had a river and a brook embossed on it with a turquoise glaze—clearly these had been handmade by or for the proprietors. The table centerpiece was constructed of three Navajo chickens, brightly painted in yellow, red and black with white polka dots, their straw tails pointing in different directions.

No one spoke at the beginning of breakfast; even Walter was silent, though looks were exchanged. River and Brook had made a splendid meal of French toast with local berry sauce and maple syrup, ham, bacon and orange juice and strong coffee. As I'd noted before, it was an odd relationship between B&B host and guest, half hotelier, half old family friend. Seeming not to notice that six places were set for breakfast, Ned, with his usual gracefulness, asked the proprietors if they would join us, and asked if there was any way he could help out. This was just the invitation the proprietors needed to cross the line over to valued family friend, and they talked at us through breakfast, though greeted mostly with chewing sounds and monosyllabic replies.

Here's the information that they imparted, with the speed of someone whose duct-tape-over-the-mouth for three days had just been loosened: That Grants (their town) was a wonderful gateway to Chaco Canyon— though the tourists hadn't seemed to understand that yet—and that Chaco Canyon was a wonderful mystical place where they tried to go every year at the spring and fall equinoxes to feel the harmony of the celestial and earth spirits, just as the ancient Pueblo peoples or Anasazi did a millennium ago from their observatories, where light from the sun and stars played on ancient symbols—and wasn't the spring equinox soon?—that they made their own stoneware, and some was for sale, and would we like to buy some? that Grants and especially Gallup where we were going, were centers for the illicit trade in archeological items scavenged at the enormous digs in Chaco Canyon, and the items were sold to collectors, smugglers and thieves; that Chaco Canyon was about two hours from here; that at this time of year it was treacherous with mud that would sink a car, or cold enough with ice to blow out tires; that Gallup was full of mostly Navajo

Indians who lived on their Reservations, and came to Gallup to spend their money; that they had never heard of Simon Yahouti or his research.

Having imbibed a wonderful fortifying meal and several mugs of strong Kona coffee, ground by hand and made with purified water, I was in excellent shape to start my day. Former lawyer-yuppie-hippies certainly know how to live!

Before the meal was officially over, I excused myself to the front room to call E.J. and check in. Cell phones don't work well in this part of the country, so I relied on the old fashioned landline telephone and my 60-minute calling card. It was only 6 a.m., but E.J. was already up.

"Where are you?" said E.J., and "Have you found Simon yet?"

"We're in Grants, heading west to Gallup. We're on Simon's trail, but haven't reached him yet. He wasn't at Acoma, but he has a room in Gallup so we're heading there."

"Schaeffer," started E.J. slowly. "When Dorothea died yesterday, the crime became murder and the Santa Fe police and the San Juan Pueblo sheriff are on the case. Simon is the chief suspect. He could be dangerous, if you find him."

"Do you think it's possible that Simon could do that?"

E.J. said, "I wouldn't have thought so, Schaeffer, but husbands are always suspect number one, and with good reason statistically," she added sadly. "I'm glad I've had only one so far, and it may be my last. And you, Schaeffer, are two enough?"

I shrugged. "Never say never," I said. I didn't have time for far-ranging matrimonial speculations just now. "How are things at the center?"

"Oh, I don't know. The fellows are trying to go on with their work. Terry Franchot is actually making himself useful, in a smarmy, officious sort of way. He's taking over some of Ned's responsibilities for now and working on more secure access."

"That reminds me, E.J., why on Earth did you saddle me with the motley crew of Ned, Walter and Veronica?"

"I had no choice—honest, Schaeffer. Veronica is on the Board; she's my boss. And I wanted you and Ned. I trust you. About Walter, though, I'm not really sure how he slipped in."

"Well, he almost slipped off the cliffs of Acoma yesterday. I don't really get Walter."

"Nothing to get, I think. He's on an obsessive quest for eternal life.

Don't worry about him. He's oblivious; he just lets things go by."

"By the way, have you heard anything further from Count von Spanish Dracula?"

"Ah. Commander Philip Gomez-Ibañes. Yes, he checked in on me once... made vague threats. Suggested that I would be fired from the center and that he would have to take matters into his own hands."

"Hmm. Does the Count have any henchmen?"

"You know that he's part of an elite fraternity of pure-blood Hispanics, deriving from Spain. It's half a Hispanic Booster club—like when they received King Philip of Spain with an elaborate dress ceremony—and half a vigilante group. I wouldn't be surprised if henchmen were involved; it wouldn't be like the Order of Spain group to sully their own swords with the mixed blood of riff-raff. Why do you ask?"

"I may have run into a henchman-type in Acoma and was wondering whose hench he was. He's very large and aggressive. Since we didn't formally exchange business cards, I've named him Bubba. I guess that would be El Gordo in New Mexico." I was gratified to hear the regular E.J. throaty laugh. "Well, I need to go...I know your center doesn't need more bad publicity," I said. "Any last thoughts?"

"Find Simon before anyone else does, that's number one, and try to find the Oñate vessel. The center might not survive the loss of this blasted artifact. But Schaeffer, be safe. You know I care about you all more than about a piece of pottery."

I got to the table as the goodbyes were being said, subdued on the part of the guests, bubbly on the part of the lonely hippies. It was really a wonderful B&B, and I hoped the hippies had found their lost city of gold.

I offered to drive first and I headed out the long entry road from Cibola. Ned and I were wary of each other this morning, and he had taken the back seat of the Volvo. Walter climbed in with me and started doing deep breathing exercises. I waved goodbye to the llamas in the pens at the side of the road.

"That was a very good breakfast," Walter began conversationally. "Do you know that every long-lived person claims to have special eating habits that prolonged his or her life?"

"Mmm," I said, thinking to myself that there's a razor-thin edge between research, hobby and mania.

"Yes, a lot of them have to do with breakfast. Some say they eat it every day, others avoid it. More often it's a special food, like an American woman who died at age 115, saying that she sprinkled vinegar on all her food and ate plenty of pickles."

"That sort of makes sense, Walter," I said. "Preservatives and all."

"Yes, much better sense than the woman from Belarus, who lived to be 113 and attributed her age to the village daily diet of home-made sausages, pork fat and bread."

At the end of the Cibola road, on the way back to the highway, I filled up the gas tank at a little convenience store with one self-service pump outside. When I went in to pay, I also stocked up on a case of bottled water, packaged peanut butter cookies and six dark chocolate Hershey bars. I wanted to be ready for whatever came our way.

As I pulled away from the store, I noticed a red low-rider tearing away in front of me and leaving a cartoon-like cloud of dust. I thought I caught sight of Bubba/El Gordo in the driver's seat, but if so, why wasn't he following me instead of getting ahead of me? Scary, yes; intelligent, no, I thought. Until I saw him waiting for me at the on-ramp to Gallup, his revolver dangling casually out the window in his left hand, the threatening skull-crossed tattoo on his forearm, winking at me with evil intent.

We drove to Gallup along Route 40 West, the sun rising behind us. It was the beginning of a remarkably clear and sun-filled day, and we raced across the flat straight mesa filled with incipient hope. I was sure that we'd find Simon in Gallup and end this unfortunate chase. There wasn't much along the road—an Indian Casino every now and again; a small Pueblo town nestled away from the highway, occasionally centered by a simple white stone church, a little like the one at Acoma.

The only small fly in the proverbial ointment was El Gordo in the low-rider. He seemed to have a companion—probably an equally well-mannered and nicely accoutered friend riding shot gun, quite literally; they were following us at a discrete distance. I considered briefly whether it was possible to lose him.

"Veronica," I said to my silent companion, "would you please check the map to see what alternate routes there are to Gallup?"

She turned full upon me as if I had asked to be included in her will. Few had the audacity to request Veronica's assistance. But without responding, she checked the map and responded coldly, "You can take the train, of course, or use old Route 66, which runs parallel to Route 40, but keeps coming back to it. Why do you want to know?"

Was Veronica innocent, then, of my low-rider pal? And if so, should I clue her and the others in?

"There seems to be someone following us," I said. "Red low-rider; driver heavy set. Companion not in plain view." Everyone looked back all at once.

"Can you all be a little more obvious?" It was too late. As I glanced back at the rear view mirror, I saw El Gordo, unsmiling, wave at me and then draw a finger across his throat in pantomime.

"Great," I said. "We've made contact. I don't think we can lose him anyhow on the roads he knows. But I have an idea: when we get to Gallup, let's split up to look for Simon. Bubba—I call him Bubba because he looks like a linebacker to me—and his little friend can't follow all of us." No comment from the peanut gallery. "So what are the places we should look in Gallup?" I handed my guidebook and map back to Veronica. She accepted it ungraciously.

Ned spoke up for the first time. "I guess we can rule out the FBI office. That's where Tony Hillerman's detectives usually go in Gallup."

"Thank you for that literary analysis," I said dryly. "We've now officially ruled out the FBI office."

Ned laughed briefly, not noticeably lightening the atmosphere. "Well, we don't know where Simon lives, but there's a strip downtown with a few stores where everyone goes. Didn't the lady you met at the Casino, Schaeffer, say that Simon worked at the old, turn of the century Richardson's trading post / pawn shop / collectible store? I'll check that out."

"And next to Richardson's is Zimmerman's," Walter piped up, "a Western clothier store. It was founded in the 1880s, and Mr. Zimmerman's son is still alive. I'll check that store out. Maybe Mr. Zimmerman junior is walking about the premises somewhere and would consent to an interview."

"I'll take Earl's," I said. Earl's was a famous eatery in Gallup, much recommended by my guidebook. "It's always open and everyone goes there to eat. There's a program for Indians to sell their handmade jewelry to customers."

"Well," said Veronica with a sigh, "As a Board member, I have been entrusted with this mission as well, and I will do my part. I have some old acquaintances at the El Rancho Hotel. It's rather grand—where John

Wayne and Henry Fonda stayed when they made movies out here—down at the heels a little now. I know the manager."

"Okay, I plan to park somewhere central, and then we scatter to our prospective places. No matter who or what we find, we meet back at Veronica's El Rancho Hotel in one hour."

It was only 10:30 a.m. when I exited the highway and drove into Gallup. I'm sure that Tony Hillerman knew it better than I did, but to an outsider, it was a pretty rundown, unpleasant place. It should have had a sign that said, "Gallup: The Home of Indian Exploitation." It was really a sad-looking place. The Santa Fe Railroad and Amtrak ran the whole length of the town, which put everything on the wrong side of the tracks. The town's offerings seemed to embody all the many ways for Indians to be parted from their weekly paychecks, most unseemly, alcohol in many forms, gambling and slovenly run-down motels that rented by the day or hour. For the inevitable day-after remorse, there was more of same, plus the ubiquitous pawnshops. Not a place, I thought, to linger. Maybe I wasn't seeing the scenic side.

I parked at a meter near the tracks, and we all eased out of the Subaru and shook our limbs. Oddly, there was no sign of the low-rider. We walked back toward the center of Main Street. Following our plan, Ned peeled off at the first store on the corner, Richardson's, a large and handsome establishment, with hand-crafted saddles, hand-worked silver belts and turquoise jewelry in the window, much of which looked very old. My heart sank when Ned went in the door. Would I see him again?

Feeling foolish, my emotions exposed at least to myself, I watched with equanimity as Walter, rather cleverly, remained outside the second place, Zimmerman's store, which also had a real old-fashioned look to it, pretending to study the window displays. Zimmerman's advertised "apparel and dry goods." These turned out to be stacks of cloth and such. I'd always wondered what "dry goods" were; all goods that were not wet seemed to cover a lot of territory.

It was a ways to El Rancho Hotel, but still on the main street on the edge of town, Veronica turned into the hotel lobby, complaining as she went, that it had clearly gone down hill since John Wayne's last visit. I looked in briefly and found it exactly as Hollywood would have wanted an outpost hotel in Indian territory to look. It had a huge, dark lobby, all of wood, with a large roaring hearth fire on the far wall. Deer antlers were mounted on a wooden balcony and staircase, perfect either for looking out for people below or making an appropriately grand entrance. The floor was paved in authentic Mexican orange tile, and great stuffed leather chairs with Navajo Pendleton blankets were nested in the lobby's many alcoves. I could also see several wooden picture frames on the walls holding faded black and white photos, but I couldn't make out who was in them. As I slipped back onto the street, Veronica was talking imperiously to the concierge. Perhaps her attitude would get us results.

As for me, I ambled along the street as the map suggested, looking like a tourist—and there were a handful of them—looking for somewhere to eat. I finally stumbled across Earl's at the end of the street. It was impossible to miss, being the only establishment I'd seen for blocks that looked like it was actually in business. There were also the big signs with huge pictures of food touting Earl's length of time in business. Large pictures of food may not be a subtle strategy for luring customers, but it was apparently effective. A long line was forming on the left side of a white-washed adobe building, but the line was moving fairly quickly. In line mostly with large Indian families, I ran a gauntlet of Indians selling their hand-made jewelry and other items. A paper brochure handout explained how to tell real Native jewelry from that made in the Philippines (!), but it was unclear to me how to be sure. The only real way was to buy directly from the artist or artisan, it said. I was tempted by several items, but finally struck up a brief conversation with a matronly lady with long braids who was selling necklaces of leather with a small turquoise piece at the end set in silver. "Turquoise," she said to me mildly "is good protection. It keeps bad luck away."

I'll take a dozen, I thought, but said I would take one at a reasonable ten dollars. I also received a little note from the artist, called Sally Mankiller, something like a taxi receipt certifying she was a Navajo Indian and that the silver and turquoise were real.

"Thank you," I said, "I'll wear it right now if you'll help me put it on."

Sally Mankiller nodded and I knelt down so that she could fasten it around my neck. I wondered whether the "Mankiller" was an honorific or merely a family name. She seemed reasonably harmless in her later years.

"Ms. Mankiller," I began when I was safely festooned with my turquoise charm, "I'm looking for a friend of mine. Can you help me?"

She nodded her eyes down.

"His name is Simon Yahouti" I continued.

"He is not Navajo," said my informant.

"Yes, I believe that he may be a Hopi."

"Move along," said my erstwhile friend, and looked down at her jewelry in front of her.

If I had said that he was Mussolini's nephew, I couldn't have made a greater faux pas. Oh well, I wouldn't make that particular mistake again. Ancient grudges seem to be universal and inexplicably do not decrease with time.

I had been looking out for Bubba and Co. at intervals and was somewhat disconcerted to have lost them. Were they following my untrustworthy teammates? Or did they know where to find Simon better than we did? Meanwhile, the line was moving up inexorably to the many booths and hearty platters of New Mexican fare inside Earl's.

Never one to pass up an indigenous meal, or actually a meal of any kind, I ordered a Platter One, which seemed to have pretty much everything on it: soft tacos, crisp tacos, beef and bean enchiladas, beans, rice, and a sopapilla—a warm puff pastry on the side.

"Green or red chile?" asked my waiter, who looked about 12.

"Which is hotter?" I asked innocently.

"It varies," my waiter replied, "But here green chiles are milder. Why not order "Christmas" and I'll put a little of both on the side."

"Christmas it is," I said. "And a Diet Coke, please. I'm watching my weight." My young waiter laughed, I guess because I had just ordered the gargantuan "Platter One" with everything on it.

New Mexican cuisine, I was told daily, is subtler than what Americans think of as Tex-Mex. Certainly it was delicious, flavorful and filling. Both the red and green chile salad on the side proved too fierce for my inexperienced palate, and I soothed it with a wonderful sopapilla—an airy dessert of fried dough served with honey—at least at Earl's.

Of course, I wasn't idle while I gorged myself—that is, fortified myself—for trials to come. I queried my young waiter for information on Simon and, having none, he went back to the kitchen to inquire. In addition to good food, Earl's had entertainment: a slow but steady line of Indian artisans from the line outside were walking through the restaurant with one or two pieces of jewelry on black velvet covered cardboard. They didn't bother anyone who didn't express interest and because most of the diners were locals anyway, no one paid them much attention.

As I was savoring the last of my sopapilla, dipping it into the honey on my plate, Sally Mankiller came toward me in the slow procession through the restaurant. At first, I thought she wouldn't even look at me, but as she came by, she stopped as if to show me a necklace and said quietly,

"I asked about Simon Yahouti for you."

"Thank you," I said. I guessed that female solidarity had trumped inter-tribal hostilities.

She nodded. "He's here right now," she said, and she pointed to the cash register at the front of the dining room.

"Thank you, Ms. Mankiller," I said hurriedly, and left a twenty-dollar bill on the table. Simon looked like his photo: a tall young man of thirty-five or so with longish dark hair. He was leaving the restaurant as she spoke. I jumped up, and called his name. He turned briefly and looked at me full on and then bounded out the door with great agility. As I made it to the front door after him, I saw him run down an alleyway behind the restaurant. I followed as fast as I could.

As I tried to overtake Simon, I was horrified to hear the sound of someone running after me. I turned my head to look and found that that someone was Bubba. My, that large muscle-bound man with a beer belly could barrel along when he had to. His gun was out of its holster, ready to shoot. Not surprisingly, Bubba overtook me in a few seconds, but I was astonished that he didn't try to stop me at all. He was after Simon, and I was leading the way for him. For some reason, perhaps because of my last encounter with Bubba, or the fact that he was such a freeloader and I was doing his work for him, this insight infuriated me and gave me a mighty adrenaline rush. Relaxing and sinking as I went, which is no small feat, I dashed down the unfamiliar alley, overtook Bubba, got in front of him, and turned to face him. He, furious in turn, ran at me—while I "rolled back," a T'ai Chi move where you basically get out of the way while the assailant lunges forward and trips over your cleverly placed right foot. Right on cue, Bubba lunged at me with all his force, missed me, tripped and fell face forward with a great thud!

While he was trying to pick up his heavy frame, I kicked away his gun and jumped on him. I was looking to hit him with a knuckle fist with the middle knuckle jutting forward at a pressure point where his ch'i was most vulnerable, say at the neck, but such a point was hard to find in that combo of muscle and blubber. Still in a fury, I pummeled his face and shouted at him, "Who are you? Who sent you? What are you doing?"

Bubba, though dazed from the fall, started to turn over and get up, preparing no doubt to annihilate me with one blow as he would an annoying insect.

In some ways, it may have been fortunate that I didn't get to see the final act. The last thing I can remember is being hit on my head, not by Bubba, but from behind, with a hard object. The lights went out.

CHAPTER 17

"What subtle strange message had come to her out of the West?"

—*Zane Grey*, Riders of the Purple Sage

WHEN I CAME TO—fuzzily—at some indeterminate time later, I was not sure whether I had gone to Hades or to the Elysian Fields. On the one hand, the back of my head hurt to beat the band. On the other, my aching head and shoulders were being cradled in Ned's strong arms. His face was close to mine, and his right cheek nestled against mine as he talked softly into my ear. He said soothing words that a horse whisperer might say, and I was comforted by his tone before I could make sense of his meaning.

"Please wake up, Schaeffer," he said softly and imploringly.

This was lovely. I fluttered my eyelids slightly to show encouragement for more soft words.

"I'd feel terrible if you aren't all right," Ned continued in a soothing, but imploring vein. "I'll never forgive myself if you don't recover…" Interesting. I began to think more clearly. Concern and affection, fine, but guilt? What did he have to be guilty about? Had he hit me over the head?

Yes, it was coming back to me. I had spotted the elusive Simon, running from Earl's restaurant. Then I had run after him, was tackled by Bubba, and had unceremoniously been knocked out by some unknown person from behind. With a sense of greater urgency and a deep cleansing breath, I opened my eyes and struggled to a half-sitting position resting on my elbows. Ned still supported me, on one knee, and my first look up was rewarded with his tentative but radiant smile. He gave me an involuntary squeeze, which moved my head rather too swiftly for comfort and then drew back to look at me with pleasure. I hazarded a small smile and, looking beyond Ned, took in the hovering figures of Veronica and Walter. "Thanks for finding me, guys. I'm okay, I think."

"Well, that's a relief," said Veronica emphatically, sounding annoyed, either with my being a delay and a burden, or by the fact that I was still alive. Walter clucked at me with concern and said that I should avoid head injuries in the future since they correlated negatively with living to be over 100. I replied somewhat tartly that in the future I would make every effort not to be hit from behind.

As my companions were helping me up and over to our parked Subaru several streets away, I remembered everything. I told them my story, halt-ingly, coming to the sad ending of how I practically had Simon in my grasp before I was felled by an unknown assailant. I explained how Simon was also being pursued by our friend Bubba and by a third person, and that I didn't know if his other pursuers caught up with him, but that Simon was fast and agile. My colleagues listened to my story, and Ned offered me bottled water and chocolate to help me regain my strength.

"But how did you find me?" I asked. "And did you see who hit me? And did you see Bubba? And Simon? Did you catch up to him?"

They explained that they had gone to Earl's when I didn't show up at the El Rancho Hotel at the appointed time, and that the waiter had told them that I had run out of the restaurant, bolting after an Indian, into the alley alongside the building. They had gone down the alley and found me lying there unconscious, with no one else in sight.

I groaned. Had Simon gotten away or been taken by Bubba and his friend? And if Simon had gotten away, where was he now?

"You know," Ned said, "All is not lost. You, Schaeffer, can now iden-tify Simon, and I—I also got some information at Richardson's, where Si-mon works part time to finance his archeological-astronomic explorations. A friend of his there told me what Simon has been looking for and where he's been looking for it." Ned waited while we took in the information with appreciation and renewed hope. "I don't suppose you, Veronica or Walter, were able to find out anything?" he asked with feigned modesty.

"Not really," Veronica said sharply. "Just tell us what you found out."

We all turned again to Ned. "Well," he said, enjoying his superior knowledge, "Simon usually works for a few weeks or a month at a time in Richardson's and as soon as he has saved some money, he goes out into the desert with camping equipment for a month or so, always around the ruins of Chaco Canyon. He's looking for an archeological site—one of hun-dreds—that hasn't been excavated yet, but that he's sure it's there and that it houses the kind of astronomical structure that some of the other great houses in the ruin have. That is, certain religious sites in the Chaco Canyon are complex and constructed to let the ancient Pueblo peoples know exactly the moment of the solstice and the equinox. Apparently, at exactly those times the sunlight falls on a manmade indicator—a small window in a sacred stone or a special carving that designated sun readers knew how to interpret. But Simon is looking for something else. He thinks the light of the sun at the spring or fall equinox will point him to a discovery that he's been looking for since he was a graduate student, for about 10 years."

"What sort of discovery?" Veronica asked with interest and rapacity.

Ned shook his head. "His friend at Richardson's didn't know. Simon would never tell him, but he did tell his friend where he was going to look next. The site is in Chaco Canyon National Historic Park, somewhere northeast of the excavated ruins of Casa Bonita."

Walter had pulled out the map in my guidebook. His red Van Dyke beard moved side to side in a series of negative nods. "Not to be a nay-sayer," he began.

"Then don't be," Veronica interrupted curtly.

"But Chaco Canyon is vast. It's virtually impossible that we could find a lone camper out there."

Ned and I looked at one another.

"Well, I'm going to try," I said. "You guys can take the train back if you want to. I'm not giving up now. I told E.J. that I would bring back the Oñate vessel and I intend to do it," I said with a great deal more certainty than I felt.

A period of quiet consternation followed.

"I'll come with you, Schaeffer," Ned said. "I don't want to let you go in alone. Chaco Canyon is pretty wild this time of year and, besides, you seem to attract trouble."

Ah, flattery. Was Ned really concerned about me? Was he hoping to help E.J. in order to make up for the artifact piracy of his youth? Or was he determined to get the Oñate vessel for Veronica as the price of her silence?

I preferred the first two motivations, but had to concede that the third was a strong possibility and that Ned was at the least conflicted in his role as friend or foe.

As soon as Ned had decided, Veronica immediately determined that she would continue with us as well. Jealousy and greed, and possibly the thrill of the hunt were probably on her mind. I could see in the handsome structure of her animated face, the beauty that often hid under an immobile, impervious mask.

What really surprised me was that Walter, though somewhat fearful, was also game. This was not a trip calculated to add years to his life so I had to wonder why he was so keen. Was he afraid—after being pushed off the cliff at Acoma—to travel back alone? Or had his adventurous side finally been roused? Not likely.

I would just as soon have gone on by myself rather than with these three largely unhelpful, sometimes untrustworthy and possibly malevolent fellow travelers. Well, I made a mental exception for Ned, who had cradled my bruised head so carefully and who had found—at least he claimed to have found—Simon's destination.

So we buckled in and started on the ride back to Chaco Canyon. Ned offered to drive first, and I sat next to him up front. The first leg retraced our route on Interstate 40, this time East back towards Albuquerque. It was a straight shot back through Thoreau and Milan (yes, the New Mexicans were fanciful with place names) and just before returning to Grants, with its Cibola B&B, we turned left on 605 North, still a good road, still following the guidebook map. We then turned left again on 509 North and left again at the town of White Horse, which was really just a fork in the road with a couple of houses. This part of the trip took about 90 minutes; the rest of the way to Chaco Canyon, just 20 miles away, the book warned, would take over an hour, how much over depended on the condition of the one lane dirt road into the park. Bad conditions included very dry or frozen ground, which would do damage to the tires, or very wet and muddy ground, which would cause a car to get stuck or spin off the road. Given the range of bad conditions, it seemed likely that good conditions, whatever they were, were not the norm.

Chaco Canon is a National Park and a World Heritage site. These designations make it sound safe and inviting, with friendly park rangers patrolling and snack bars with soft drinks at frequent intervals. But actually, as my guide book said, Chaco Canyon covers 34,000 acres and at most points is at least 30 miles from the nearest paved road. It is high desert, covered with sage brush and arroyos, the dry stream beds that can flood at a moment's notice. It has well over a thousand archeological sites, most not yet excavated; and it's home to coyotes, bobcats, vultures, Western Prairie rattlesnakes, bats, owls and scorpions.

There was no question what road conditions we were looking at. Although the weather was dry and blustery, it had recently rained hard and drenched the road in front of us, showing deep muddy ruts and large muddy puddles, small lakes actually, as far as the eye could see. It was not an inviting prospect and I had to admit that I wondered whether the green Subaru and our motley crew were up to it.

However, I took a deep breath and suggested we go in. I offered to drive for the first stretch. Ned demurred and said he should keep the wheel, that he was an expert on such roads from his early archeological days. But I insisted. This really was my show.

I can't really give you an adequate idea of how wild and desolate Chaco Canyon was this time of year—it had to be off-season—as we ventured on to the road north into the excavation area. Although it was just 3 o'clock in the afternoon, the sky was dark with storm clouds, which blew low around us with impetuous ferocity. The clouds were as beautiful as any I had ever seen, sweeping through that great Western sky over flat land to every horizon, but they seemed menacing. On either side of the road, the ground lay flat, or in small mounds covered with rocks and pebbles, either deposited by the odd natural forces that shaped the New Mexican landscape, or possibly left from ancient Pueblo dwellings. Less than a fifth of the area had been excavated but it was assumed that everything was evidence of a once glorious civilization of the ancient Pueblo, the ancestors of the Hopi and the current Pueblo Indians. The shrubbery that dotted the landscape was very low tufts of desert grasses, tiny pine-like dwarf plants, nothing above a foot high to break the vast horizontal line of sky and Earth. The clouds continued to build and destroy huge castles in the sky in an ever-changing ominous display.

Once we started on the road, however, we had a better idea of the menace ahead. The dirt road had turned to mud, which oozed and squished around our tires and sprayed up on the windshield a half an inch thick. I turned the wipers on, but it was nearly a lost battle at every turn. We only hoped that the wiper fluid would hold out, or we would soon be encased with mud.

I drove on slowly; the road was at least straight, very flat and there were, not surprisingly, no other cars either coming or going our way. The greatest danger lay in the little lakes of mud every half mile or so, which I went through cautiously, trying not to either spin off the road or get us stuck in the mud.

Naturally, I looked ahead for signs that a car or cars had been there before us and the tire ruts looked very fresh to me—signs of recent travelers into the area.

We were going first into the heart of Chaco Canyon, to check in at the one ranger station, and ask if Simon or "friends" of Simon had stopped by. From there, we were going to drive along the beaten path to Casa Bonita, one of the grandest of the excavated religious centers with large and numerous kivas, the sacred ceremonial spaces, often circular, and sometimes below ground, where the priests of the religion made contact with the gods of the Earth.

After the 20 miles of sloshing and sliding through the viscous muck, we arrived at the ranger station, a low circular adobe building encircled by a small parking lot. It was completely empty, except for a yellow jeep with the black letters, RANGER on the side. Signs in the lot also warned us that there was no food available in the Chaco Canyon Historical Park and no camping provisions.

We all got out of the Subaru to inquire inside and weren't surprised to see that our vehicle was completely coated with mud over every inch except for the parts of the windshield accessible by windshield wipers, which were rather smeared with mud.

The ranger (his badge read RANGER GREEN) at the information desk inside was equally surprised to see us and inquired which way we had come in. We told him that we had come in through the southern road and he informed us that we must have been the last car in since the road had subsequently been closed to the public as impassable; the northern road in, he informed us, had been closed since yesterday as a minivan with a family from Australia had gotten stuck in the mud and had to be evacuated by helicopter.

"Actually, we didn't have any trouble getting here," I said with a quiet pride, lying through my teeth. "But I suppose the roads are worse off the main route."

The Ranger was definitely into the adventurous side of his position and declared with enthusiasm that only a fool on a mission would venture off the main road deeper into the park. He went on to add that "Park" was something of a misnomer as it really consisted of miles of badlands, no food, no water, minimal natural shelter, and a number of hungry wild animals in search of scarce food.

"Yes, that's what we were told, and it's why we're concerned about our friend Simon. We have reason to think that he may be in Chaco Canyon."

"That wouldn't be Simon Yahouti would it?" said the chatty Ranger starved for conversation.

"It would!" I said with just enough surprise in my voice.

Happy to show off his knowledge, he went on: "He was here just a couple of hours before you. I see him all the time, you know. He had his old beat-up black Jeep. I guess you'd know that." I nodded as though I did.

"But he wasn't dragging his horse trailer this time. Lucky thing. Simon comes out here, oh, three or four times a year and camps out for weeks. I don't know how he does it in all kinds of weather. He's interested in the solstices and the equinoxes, you know. How the sun hits these certain structures in the canyon, so that ancient Pueblo people who built Chaco Canyon—we used to call them Anasazi, since this was the name the Navajo's gave them—"

"You were saying?" I urged him on.

"Oh, yes. The ancient Pueblo people who built the massive structures which radiate out from Chaco Canyon like spokes of a wheel, sort of like the Roman Empire, had sun-readers who would watch the sun as it fell through certain windows, and they could tell the solstices and equinoxes with precision. Very important for planting and harvesting, you know, and for rituals and prayers, of course. All of the structures have at least one kiva—usually a large, round room under the first floor where the initiated invoked the gods of Earth, where the Pueblos believe they all came from originally. The small hole in the kiva, in the sacred origin myths, is called the siapu."

The ranger was now on a roll, which I found rather informative, though time was a-wasting in our search for Simon.

"In some of the kivas there are pictographs (that's writing on the wall) or petroglyphs (that's carving on the wall) that depict ancient celestial phenomena. One looks like the birth of a giant supernova. From the ancient pictures it appears to have been visible for several days, around the year 1000 A.D.

I turned to the others, "Can you gather up supplies while I talk with Mr. Green? Anything we might need, but definitely more water and some blankets."

"Ranger Green," I said leaning my elbow on his counter confidentially, "Do you know where exactly Simon went, and what he's been looking for?"

"Well, he wouldn't like it if I told anyone, but seeing as you're his friends, you know, there's so much more unexcavated ground in Chaco, and having studied archeology and pictographs and the like, your friend Simon is convinced that there are many more ancient pictures, probably petroglyphs, to be found. He also believes that there are some from the time of Christ. He's sure of it, really, though nothing has been found as early as that time as yet."

"Do you think he's right?"

"Well, Simon is a little odd, but he's smart and he's patient, and—now, really, don't tell him I told you this—"

"Of course not," I nodded.

"But today, he came in very excited. He said that he had the key to the puzzle he had been searching for."

"Did he tell you any more?"

Suddenly, Ranger Green became suspicious. I looked as innocent and friendly as I could, cupping my hands under my chin and looking up at him in what I hoped was an admiring way.

"What did you say your name was?" he asked in a more official way.

"Schaeffer Cornell," I replied. "Why do you ask?" I was the sweet blush of innocence itself.

"Oh well, never mind…what was I saying?"

"Simon came in today excited about some discovery," I prompted, trying not to sound too eager.

"Yes. He said he had come into possession of an artifact from a very early period, and if he could place the piece in just the right position, in a dig he had been working on, the alignment of the sun would yield something significant."

I was hopeful for more information, but that was all Ranger Green provided. When he resumed his tale, it was just embellishment—how excited Simon was, what supplies he took with him.

Finally, I asked if he knew where Simon had gone and whether—more to allay his suspicions more than anything else—he would lead us there.

"I couldn't abandon my post, Ms. Cornell, is it? They need me here in case of an emergency."

The "they" was a vague reference to be sure, but he made his apology with a great deal of pride in his work.

"You can find Simon, I think, if you go off the main route at Casa Bonita and then go due east until you see his Jeep. His excavation, he told me, is about twenty miles in. The road is really bad, though. I warned Simon about going out there tonight. He just laughed at me. He reminded me that tonight is the spring equinox."

Omygosh.

"Has anyone else been by the Ranger Station tonight?" I finally remembered to ask.

"In these conditions? You've got to be kidding," Ranger Green said with an ironic smile.

"Ned," I said, as my traveling companions lined up at the counter to buy our supplies. "You'd better go back and buy us a compass."

CHAPTER 18

"Go ahead. You'll thank me later."

—Adrian Monk, Detective

WELL, WE PILED BACK INTO THE SUBARU, brimming with camping accoutrements, like freeze-dried lasagna ("just add water, stir, taste, and puke"), but we did have lots of water and blankets, and the compass which I put up front on the dashboard. Expecting to be nominated by popular acclaim to drive again, as I had performed so ably on the first leg of the trip, I began to open the door to the driver's seat, only to find Walter, at the driver's door, contesting the role.

"I'd like to take the wheel for a bit. If you don't mind," said Walter with one of his silly, half-moon smiles. We were all surprised, since Walter had never offered to do his share of anything before and had been, relatively speaking, even more useless after his fall off the cemetery cliff at Acoma.

"Okay," I said. "You're experienced with E.J.'s Subaru?"

"Oh, cars, like women, are all alike in the dark, and it will be getting dark if we don't hurry."

"Okay," I said again doubtfully, as Walter favored me with a wiggle of his pointy and always perfectly groomed beard, and I reluctantly handed over the key. I went around to the other side and sat next to him in the front; Veronica and Ned took the back seat. My spirits were not buoyed to see Walter search a long time for the groove in which to insert the car key, a comparatively easy first step, and then fumble around for the lights and the windshield wipers.

It was getting dark—more from the now thickening clouds overhead than the position of the sun. It was only about 4 p.m., and we had at least an hour and a half of daylight left.

Walter backed the Subaru up, and we set off to the west on a route which, I could see form Ranger Green's annotated map, made a circle tour of the major excavations. I told the others briefly what I had learned from the ranger while they had been gathering supplies. I told Walter that he should keep on the circle route till we told him to turn off. With Walter faltering at the helm, we sloshed and swerved our way to the first grand kiva complex, Casa Bonita.

As focused as I was on finding Simon, I was floored to see it, rising out of nothing in the high desert of New Mexico. It was vast, ruined structure with several kivas, surrounded by multi-storied apartment buildings on three sides. It was a thing of wonder and beauty and desolation. Many artifacts had been found here, including beautiful ceramics, silver and turquoise, and seashells and parrot feathers, which had led scholars to believe that Chaco had once been a thriving civilization and hub of commerce far and wide. Now the wind and rain had battered its deserted structures and rock, like the fallen remains of the statue of Shelley's "Ozymandias," mocking its earlier grandeur. Scholars did not really know why this grand city had been suddenly deserted, nor why the ancient Pueblos had scattered to the Pueblos we visited near Santa Fe, Albuquerque and the Hopi lands near Gallup. Some anthropologists thought that nomadic Indians such as the Navajo and Apache had invaded from the north. Others thought the disappearance of the Ancient Pueblos had to do with climate change, likely drought. Apart from Machu Picchu in the Andes and, of course, Indianapolis, most city planners had had the foresight to build on a river or other large body of water.

As we approached, I read the following from my guidebook: "The great house of Pueblo Bonito is the largest of all Chacoan structures with around 700 rooms. The view of Pueblo Bonito from the overlook trail shows the building's traditional D-shaped floor plan. An impressive feature of Pueblo Bonito is its alignment to the cardinal directions. A line drawn through the center of the half moon shape forms a precise north-south axis and the eastern half of its southern wall is aligned east-west. On the spring and fall equinoxes, the sun rises and sets in perfect alignment with this wall."

Not willing to lose any time before catching up with Simon, we stopped only briefly. The sun, such as it was, was beginning to set, adding some vibrant yellows and purples to the bottoms of the towering storm clouds. For the most part, the rain held off.

"Now, Walter," I said, as I looked carefully at our compass on the dashboard, "we are going to go due east as soon as we find a small dirt road in that direction."

A few hundred yards past the main entrance to Casa Bonita I spotted such a road, so narrow and muddy that I hoped I was mistaken. I jumped out to inspect it. Clearly it was the road Simon had taken just a few hours before. The wheel tracks were fresh in the mud. I recognized them as Jeep tracks, which I was familiar with from my own, much missed old Jeep, back at home in McLean, Virginia. The road was oozing with fresh mud which settled in great globs on my boots as I took a few steps to look around. There was nothing to see in any direction. Fired up from seeing the recent tire tread marks, I reported that we were indeed on Simon's trail, and suggested that we waste no time.

As soon as I was seat-belted in again, Walter took off on the new path so slowly that my patience was tried.

"Walter," I said, "I'd be happy to drive for a while if you're tired. It takes a lot of concentration on these roads."

"No thank you, Schaeffer. I'm doing fine. You don't want us to get stuck in this mess, do you?"

"But you're going so slowly, we're sure to be stuck," I said with exasperation. "It's like you're trying not to get there!" Walter sped up a little at that, but my words hung in the air, and echoed in my own ears. How had I been so blind? Walter was trying not to get us there. That had been his goal on this trip all along. It was Walter who had been "pushed" off the mountain top in Acoma—well, that wasn't his fault, I guess—but it was Walter who needed to stop for a drink after that and insisted on staying overnight at a bed and breakfast. Walter was either acting on orders or of his own accord, but His Silliness was obviously a man with a mission. Nothing else could explain his wanting to enter Chaco with us.

In the few minutes it took for me to process this belated insight, a new and awful thought dawned on me: if Walter really thought we were about to reach Simon at his excavation, he would have to do something drastic. I sat in dread as I realized what that something would probably be, something having to do with a car and a lot of mud. After a long silence, I looked at the odometer and noted that we had been driving due east for about 15 miles. We were five miles from finding Simon. I knew that, if my reasoning was correct, Walter would not relinquish the wheel willingly and, if I fought him for it, we could certainly lose control of the car. Therefore, I determined that I would stay alert to any unnecessary swervings, and act to right our vehicle with lightening speed.

I looked at the odometer again. We had now gone 18 miles east and were only about two miles from where we hoped to find Simon. Light was fading fast, and I checked behind me while I could still see. Veronica was dozing in the backseat. Ned was looking thoughtful. No one was following us. As I turned forward again to keep my eye on Walter, he swerved the steering wheel sharply to the left and hit the accelerator with force.

Immediately, I reached with both hands to right the skidding vehicle, at the same time kicking Walter's foot off the accelerator. We looked at each other for that kind of long moment that comes between the realization and the crash, and held our collective breaths.

With a lurch left and loud crunch, the Subaru came to rest, neatly splayed out horizontally from the road, in what felt like a low gully.

"Get out of the car, Walter," I said quietly, but firmly.

"B- but—" he sputtered, "Just let me try to get out of this."

I got out of the car to walk around it and forcibly remove Walter from the driver's seat, when I heard him willfully grind the wheels further into the dirt. By the time I had got around to the other driver's seat, Ned was also out of the car and at my side.

He angrily opened the door and snatched Walter's key, which was childishly easy. "What do you think you're doing?" Ned spoke quietly, but angrily. "Please get out. You've got us mired in the mud so deep we could all die here before we pry ourselves out."

Walter shook his head at me with a foolish smile. "Just doing my best," he clucked.

Ned and I ignored Walter now and looked with rising despair at the gully we were in. Ned offered to try driving out, but once burned, I decided it was better to try myself.

"I'll drive," I said. "You push."

By that time, Veronica had come to and demanded to know where we were and what we thought we were doing.

"Ask Walter," I said curtly. "We seem to be following his agenda."

I got into the car and pretended this was snow and ice that I'm used to, instead of mud, and tried rocking the car gently forward and backward. When I went into the forward direction, Ned and Walter, the latter in a lackluster attempt to conceal his villainy, pushed from behind. This effort had little effect on the extrication process. Then I remembered the wool blanket approach. I asked Veronica to hand me the blankets we had purchased as supplies. With a rising impatience and possible panic, Veronica fumbled about and finally handed one forward, which I passed out the window to Ned. He put it under the back wheels of the car to get traction. I carefully straightened the wheels, and we tried one last time to roll forward out of the ditch.

It was clearly hopeless. Our efforts had only managed to mire us farther into the muck, digging our own automotive grave, so to speak. I checked the odometer again. We were two miles from Simon's camp. We could certainly try to walk it. On the other hand, it was now dark and starting to get extremely cold. So I checked the gas gauge—alas, only one-third full—and it was sufficient to keep us warm in the car, using the heater prudently through the night. We'd be protected from any wild critters which, we were warned, like to hunt in Chaco Canyon after dark.

Finally, I checked the skies: the moon was now shining brightly and stars were beginning to show. On the one hand, this light made walking less hazardous; on the other, the new absence of clouds, which had swept largely away during the last hour, made radiational cooling a large factor. It could go below freezing overnight. That meant that by morning the mud would be frozen and we could chip it off our tires and maybe drive away.

I really couldn't decide what to do—walk or wait? Frankly, I didn't care what the others wanted; I'd just as soon leave them—yes, even Ned—and get this search over with. This assignment was getting old, chasing the Oñate vessel over a large, mostly muddy state and dodging feuds between Indians and Hispanics was beginning to wear on me. Why couldn't everyone just get along? Who cared what someone's great grandparents did to someone else's great grandparents? It was past time to get over it.

And I felt threatened. Bubba and Co. had assaulted me twice and seriously battered me once. And there was clearly at least one subversive in my own camp, maybe more. Heck, I was hungry, tired, and in pain from the knock on my head earlier.

These impatient thoughts led me forthwith to announce perhaps one of my worst calculated decisions.

"Team," said I firmly, when everyone was back in the car. "'Once more into the breach, my friends!'" I often quote *Henry V* when I'm agitated, "We're going to walk the last two miles to Simon's camp, starting now."

A torrent of "buts," "maybes," very good reasons why not to, and alternate suggestions greeted this announcement.

"Nevertheless," I replied decisively, and got out to gather some supplies from the trunk of the car. "I'm going with you or without you." I was putting water, some cheese, peanut butter sandwiches, chocolate bars, plus a flashlight into my tote bag when Ned came up along side of me, draping one arm around my shoulders protectively.

"I'll come with you, of course. It's all my fault anyway."

"But why is it your fault, Ned?" I asked impatiently. "I can't bear to think you're the villain of this piece. Please tell me you're not."

But at that moment, Veronica came out and Ned's arm moved quickly from around my shoulders to his side.

"Walter and I are coming with you," Veronica declared. "My boots are ruined anyway." She looked ruefully at her white, Lucchese, hand-tooled in red and white stitching, ostrich-skin boots, which had been badly splattered and caked. On such sartorial details are crucial decisions made.

"Okay," I sighed. "Grab some supplies and let's get going before we freeze out here."

Famous last words.

CHAPTER 19

"Don't count your chickens unless you actually have your hands around their necks."

—Gwendlyn Katz-Spielberg

I HAD SOME TIME TO PONDER famous last words as we trudged along the mud track leading, I hoped and believed, to Simon's excavation and Oñate's vessel. My favorites are Humphrey Bogart's "I should never have switched from scotch to martinis" and Oscar Wilde's "Either this wallpaper goes, or I go."

This kept my mind occupied for about the first quarter mile. Usually, a two-mile walk is short and invigorating; this one was more like a potato sack race. Each step mired our boots in deep mud and we had to keep pulling each other out. We ended up walking two by two, to keep the process moving. Veronica latched onto Ned; and I took the lead with our road company Judas Iscariot, to whom I was not talking.

We tried walking on the side of the road, first tracing and then avoiding the ruts of the earlier tire tracks, but to no avail. Each step was a slog and we made only halting progress.

Finally, I turned to my silent and, I thought, smug companion and asked him why he was trying to sabotage our search for Simon.

"Was I?" he said with one of his self-satisfied smiles.

Just as I was thinking of a devastating response, which would necessitate Walter's admitting everything, Walter and I both stopped short in surprise, for suddenly, our flashlights illuminated a campsite—I guess we had never really believed we would find it—that had to be Simon's. There was a small army surplus tent, slightly bigger than a pup tent; there was a small excavation site, with shovels and finer archeological tools; there was a portable chair and a table which held some clay shards and pieces of stone and adobe; there was a small dwindling camp fire; there was Simon's Jeep... but there was no Simon.

In a few moments, Veronica and Ned arrived. Also caught up short, they stared in silence.

"Veronica," I said briefly, "You rest on the chair. Walter and Ned, could you please get the fire going? I want to check the perimeters."

Too startled to speak, I guess, my three companions did as they were told, and I turned my flashlight to high beam and started to look around. Starting from the campfire and moving in concentric circles as I'd been trained to do, I quietly searched Simon's tent, then his excavation, the Jeep, and then the perimeter of the site. There was no Oñate vessel, at least not in any obvious place. There was no key to the Jeep, and there was no Simon. But someone had been there very recently. As I completed my circular inspection outside the excavation site, I came to a spot where there had clearly been a recent event. Sage brush was trampled, stones were scattered, cactus had been kicked down, footprints—of at least three kinds of boots—were abundant. If I'd had to guess, I'd have said that a violent struggle had taken place there and that—heaven help us—a body had been dragged through the mud into the desert wilderness.

As I stood there, pondering whether I should follow the tracks or return to the camp, my choice was made for me.

Tramping out of the darkness from the direction of the footprints and dragging marks, came my pursuer-in-chief, Bubba, with his gun cocked and pointed at my heart.

"We meet again, Bubba," I said, trying to stay cool.

"Why do you call me that?" he said angrily. "My name is Roberto."

"It's a compliment," I said. "Referring to your great physical size and strength."

"I don't think so," Roberto/Bubba was at my side and his hand slapped me against my face. Instinctively, I put my hand up to ease the smart. I was alone with Bubba again and way outnumbered, even if I didn't count the person who was accompanying him—the person belonging to the other set of footprints. I know that Bruce Lee and my own teacher Master Zhang could take on multiple assailants, but my T'ai Chi in the main was not up to it.

"Roberto," I said, with what I hoped was a mollifying tone, "there's no reason for us to fight. We're both looking for Simon and the Oñate vessel, right? Why don't we work together and we can split the reward?"

Roberto just slapped me hard again, this time hitting the right side of my face with the back of his hand. His signet ring was particularly painful. And this was Roberto in gently-toying-with-me mode.

"You think I'm stupid, don't you? You think I'm a stupid Mexican, don't you? I'm not. I'm Hispanic, from Spain."

I couldn't believe that this man, who beat me up every time we met, was accusing me of ethnic prejudice, as if it were the source of our incompatibility. I wanted to assure him that I had no such bias, that you had to be from around these parts a long time—many generations probably—to learn to care whether a person was of Mexican or Spanish or Indian descent. I was sure that nothing would ever make me know or care, but I had a sneaking suspicion that I wouldn't be here long enough to find out.

"Roberto," I said, stalling for time and speaking more loudly in an attempt to alert Ned and the others, "I honestly don't care whether you're a Pueblo Indian or Oñate's great-great-great grandson." I had no idea how many "greats" to throw in. "I just thought we could work together instead of beating each other up regularly." I allowed myself a little descriptive latitude on that one. Roberto clearly had done more than his share of the carnage.

I was just about to feel the palm side of Roberto's hand again, when a dark figure stepped out of the gloom and into the circle of dim light provided by my flashlight.

"You don't care, do you?" It was Commandante Philip Gomez-Ibañes, in full black Conquistador regalia, his dark cape, swirling about him like Count Dracula, his black cane picking the ground before his high black boots. "You don't care, for heritage, for ancestry, for the pure blood of a conquering race. You are nobody. You have nothing. You are nothing. I am the heir to Juan de Oñate and can trace my ancestry back directly to him. I am proud of my heritage, and I will protect it. All of it.

"You are so blind," Philip continued. "you see Oñate and his heirs merely as cruel conquerors—but we made this culture—we brought civilization, horses, spices, language, and our faith. What would these petty people be today without our laws, our language, and our God?

"Roberto understands. He is one of us. He is a Spaniard and a Penitente. He is one of us."

I was dazed and dazzled by this display of chauvinism. It was hard to believe that someone could be ruled by this passion the way Philip was. But don't we all have something we would die for—or kill for?

"Did you take the Oñate vessel from the research center? Did you hurt the docent there?"

Philip laughed a harsh laugh. "You're a fool," he said. "A foolish An-glo. It's been our fate to put up with them. No—I came too late for the vessel. If I'd gotten it then, I wouldn't be here today, would I? Actually, Si-mon took it before we got there, and Roberto may, just may, have taken out our disappointment on Simon's lovely bride. Of course, now I've found Simon."

"Where is he?" I asked, hoping at least to know before worse things happened. Where was my back-up, I wondered frantically.

Philip pointed his cane behind him into the dark of the desert. "Simon is there," he said, as if talking to a child, "and the Oñate vessel is here," he said pointing to a canvas bag in his left hand. "I'm going to show the world what Oñate was, and what I am today." He paused on this triumphant note. "Roberto," he said sharply, "Take that foolish Anglo and tie her up. Then we'll find her friends and—what shall we do with them, Roberto? You guide me in this..."

Roberto handed his gun to Philip who came closer to me and pointed the gun at me at close range while Roberto took my flashlight and tied my hands behind my back. Roberto pushed me rudely forward and marched me into the camp.

Apparently unaware of the noise outside the perimeter of the camp, Ned, Veronica and Walter were warming themselves before a now roaring fire and munching on peanut butter crackers and chocolate bars. In a few minutes, I expected they'd be singing "Kumbaya" and toasting s'mores. What great friends to have in an emergency.

They looked up, startled, as Philip greeted each by name in a falsely jovial voice. "Veronica. Ned. Walter. What a surprise to find you here." Philip kept his gun on me and nodded to Roberto, who proceeded to tie Veronica's, Ned's, and Walter's hands behind their backs.

"But not really a surprise," Philip continued heartily. "Roberto and I have been tracking your movements since you left the research center. We followed you to Acoma and yes, Walter, we saw you lower yourself off the side of the cemetery cliff."

We all looked at Walter accusingly, who shrugged with a silly and slightly hysterical smile.

"We tracked you to Gallup, where, with apologies, I was forced to "brain" you, Ms. Cornell. You were making such a dog's breakfast of Roberto's face. Yes, and we followed you here to Simon's camp. Now

Simon is no more, and I have"—he tapped the bag lovingly—"the Oñate vessel."

We stared at him and the canvas bag; we stared at each other. For the life of me, I couldn't figure out a plan. Then, I thought of something. As Philip talked on—a bit madly, I thought—I worked my foot toward a burning ember in the hopes of surreptitiously kicking something very hot in his face. It wasn't brilliant, but it was the best I could do at the time. Then, if only I could get my hands loose, and use the element of surprise, perhaps I could execute "Return to the Mountain and Embrace the Tiger," which divested of its poetic title, is more colloquially, a double whammy to the neck and the groin.

As I got that far in my thinking and maneuvering, however, Philip's cane seemed to come out of nowhere and sharply flicked away the embers.

"Roberto," Philip said peremptorily. "What should we do with them?" Roberto came up to Philip and said something softly to him. "I'm disappointed in you, Roberto. Your suggestion is not gentlemanly," Philip said with a leering smile, "and besides, such a fleshly course of action would require interminable penance. No, Roberto, just put some stakes in the ground and tie our sorry friends to them. The desert will kill them, and we won't have to."

Veronica, who had been silent thus far, now spoke up boldly when Roberto pulled her roughly aside. "Philip Gomez-Ibañes," she said, "Please tell your lackey to take his hands off me. I am a Regent of the State of New Mexico. I am a Rutherford dating back to the English settlement of Jamestown in the 17th century. I have never been so insulted in all my life."

"Ah," sighed Philip with sadness—was it mock or genuine? With a madman it's really hard to say—"For the sake of our old friendship and your illustrious pedigree, I am sorry to do this to you, Veronica, but my faith and my heritage comes first. And Roberto is not a lackey. I'll have you know that he holds the high position of Sangrimento in our Penitente circle."

"What on Earth is that?" said Veronica with admirable haughtiness, I thought, since she was now lying on her back in the mud, her arms out to the side, spread-eagled, her hands tied to two stakes, and her feet together tied to one stake. Her once-white ostrich boots were pointing pitifully upward, her fawn suede jacket mired in mud.

"That is a sacred position in our religious order," Philip said, "part of our sacrament. The modern Catholic Church does not approve, but what do we care for them? Don Juan de Oñate carried his Penitente religion proudly from Spain to Mexico to Santa Fe."

Then in a business-like manner, Philip abruptly changed course. "Tie them all up, Roberto, and we'll be off." And Philip Gomez-Ibañes took his cape and silver-headed cane, and stood silently aside with his gun pointed at close range at Ned while Roberto went to work.

Roberto was admirably quick for such a large man, and managed to tie us all up to stakes on the ground in about ten minutes. Our feet were each tied to one stake away from the fire, and our arms were tied to two stakes, not unlike a crucifixion with our heads near the fire. When it was my turn, last, Roberto pushed me roughly into the mud, and straddled me suggestively while he tied me up. When my arms were bound, he ripped open my jacket and blouse and exposed my black lace camisole to the night sky. Then he got off me and laughed nastily. I can only thank my stars that he was following orders, at least up to a point.

When we were all splayed out, just beyond touching distance around the fire, Roberto left us with a few words of warning.

"Watch out for wild animals and scorpions. Too bad the fire won't keep them away." With that, he laughed, stomped out the campfire and followed Philip into the desert, leaving us in cold and darkness. Some people really know how to have a good time.

CHAPTER 20

"How am I to get out?" asked Alice again, in a louder tone. "Are you to get out at all?" said the Footman. "That's the first question, you know."

—Alice in Wonderland *(variation)*

Y OU KNOW, A LOT OF THINGS go through your mind when you are lying on your back looking up at the stars in the clear, night sky over the high desert. I could swear that I could see the Pleiades up overhead, and the belt of Orion toward the left. You think about how many stars there actually are, which you can't see on the East Coast, where one city stretches into another with hardly any gaps in between. You think about how small you are in this vast universe and how, in the words of Rick to Ilsa in *Casablanca*, our little lives don't amount to more than a hill of beans in this crazy world. Then you think—if you're like me and can't take too much philosophizing at a stretch—what is a hill of beans anyhow? Who would make a hill of beans, and to what purpose? How big would a hill of beans be? And would they be baked beans kind of stuck together or a Juan Valdez hill of coffee beans?

These philosophical thoughts lasted maybe ten seconds. Then the thought of coffee, sustenance, warmth and the lack thereof, brought me back to the actual hideous present. Lying on your back in the desert is a great deal less romantic when your arms and legs are tied to stakes in victim position, ready for animal attack or freezing to death.

I turned my head to look at my like-positioned neighbors; we were laid out like spokes of a wheel, our heads together with Veronica's body stretched out in a line with mine on one side and Ned's on the other. Everyone was very quiet, no doubt also taking this opportunity to identify familiar constellations.

"Hello," I called out to make contact with the others. Walter and Ned turned their heads toward me. Veronica didn't move. "Are you there, Veronica?" I added.

"And where would I be?" Veronica returned crisply.

"Okay," I said trying to be positive. "We're all here and accounted for."

"I'm freezing," Veronica added. "We'll freeze out here and die of dehydration."

"There, there," I said soothingly. "We'll freeze before we dehydrate. It will take at least two days to dehydrate in this weather."

"An optimistic thought." said Ned grimly.

I thought I heard some soft whimpering from Walter's direction.

"We are not going to die," I said firmly, surprised at the sound of my own strong voice. "If we were going to die, we'd be dead by now. Shot through the head. No one wants to murder us, just slow us down a little…We are going to get out of here." I said forcefully. "Alive." I added for clarity. "We need to find Simon. And the Oñate vessel."

"Oh, God," Veronica said, "I wish I'd never heard that name."

"There are just three rules for this endeavor," I continued. "Rule No. 1 is 'No Whining.'"

Silence.

"Rule No. 2," I went on, "is 'No Whining.' I guess you know Rule No. 3." The recitation got a "harrumph" from Veronica, silence from Ned, and a cessation of whimpering from Walter.

"Good," I said. "Does anyone have any ideas?"

This question brought back the cacophony of protests one might also call "whining" if it hadn't just been banned, along the lines of "I thought you had a plan," and so forth.

"Quiet, everyone. Just checking to see if I was missing something obvious. Our goal is simple: one hand, out of eight, freed from the ropes—that sounds easy. One out of eight. Let's first see if Roberto left anyone loose."

A period followed of grunts and groans as each of us tested our upper body strength against the ropes around our wrists. Alas, Roberto had done a first-rate job. The straining against the ropes, though, momentarily warmed us up.

"Okay," I said. "Plan B: is anyone holding or wearing anything that could help loosen a rope or make contact with anyone—a knife, or an electronic device, for example, or a match?"

I was really grasping at straws here. But maybe something was in someone's coat pocket that could be shaken loose and maybe make a noise or light a flare.

For a while there was silence. Then came a piercing scream from Veronica.

"Veronica, what is it?"

Veronica was unable to speak. Crawling over her face was a hideous bug as big as my hand. In the moon and starlight, I could see its tan and brown body, gnarled and wrinkled as though made of the desert sand. Its head was ugly, with two horrible pincers seemingly coming out of each eye. Its long body plated and segmented, and arched tail were even uglier. Its plethora of spindly legs gave it speed and agility. Veronica's face was now a highway for the Arizona Bark Scorpion, the nastiest insect in these parts, according to my guidebook.

Veronica stayed perfectly still and the scorpion, tail waving, menacingly, crossed onto the ground... and then up my hand and arm and, heaven help me, under my jacket and shirt. It was horrible. I thought quickly about whether the desert scorpion's bite was deadly or merely debilitating and excruciatingly painful. I tried to recall the picture of the scorpion in my travel guide with its admonitory caption. Because I'd never planned to come within a bargepole of this nasty creature, I had stared at the picture with vicarious horror and skipped quickly over the text.

Panic was rising quickly, but it seemed crucial to stay still—it had worked for Veronica—as the insect made its way up my right arm and onto my semi-bare breast. Was it worse to be stung near my heart? I thought in fear. If it were merely a limb, at least they could amputate. As the scorpion walked over me, I raised my head slightly, and to my horror, I saw it seem to stare back at me, and wave its tail stinger menacingly in the air as though it were planning to strike. I closed my eyes quickly, waiting for the inevitable and finally, finally, remembering the ever-important first principal of T'ai Chi, "Relax and Sink." I put my tongue to the top of the roof of my mouth to let the ch'i flow more freely, and I began to breathe quietly, softly and slowly.

I opened my eyes again and saw the scorpion transfixed and still staring back at me. After a long moment it turned tail, as it were, and continued a tortuous walk down my left arm, my left hand and out the sleeve of my jacket. I lay there and began to sweat, even in the cold, in a delayed reaction with tears forming in my eyes. 'No Whining,' I had to remind myself silently.

As the sweat froze quickly over my cold skin, I decided we really needed a plan now for getting out of here or at least for surviving the night in the hopes that someone might—and I mean *might*—find us in time, because we were definitely in an out-of-the-way spot. Maybe Ranger Green would come after Simon when he didn't show up... but no, Simon was often away for weeks at a time. They'd probably find our decaying bodies in June.

"Colleagues," I said solemnly, when I was in control of my panic sufficiently to speak again. No one answered me as before. "Do any of us have anything reachable that would help us be noticed or get help?"

I thought through my own inventory. My handbag was not close by; I had no idea where I had dropped it. I was wearing a watch, but it was a low-tech one, with a round face, hands and number, with no beepers, cameras, cell phones or other handy gadgets. I strained to look at the time and found it was only 11:35 p.m. Many hours of night time to go.

"Veronica," I said, "Ladies first. I have nothing in reach except a simple useless watch. What about you? Might you have a mirror available, for instance? We could use it to signal for help when the sun comes up."

"No, Schaeffer, I'm not excessively vain. I do not have a mirror accessible when I'm tied up on my back in the desert about to freeze."

"Ned?" I asked, beginning to lose hope.

"Nothing, Schaeffer."

"Walter?" I asked, not expecting much.

"Well, nothing really. But I do have some Cafe Longevity special elixir in my signet ring."

"What's that?" we all said in various ways. "What's in it? What is it? Can you get it out?"

"I'm not really sure, really." Walter said haltingly. "It has some minerals in it—you know, boron, mercury, chromium and phosphorous. I'm supposed to take a bit if I'm feeling weak, but I can't get my hand anywhere near my mouth," he finished unhappily.

Brain freeze was definitely setting in, and I mean the physical kind, so I needed to use my dwindling mental powers sooner rather than later.

"I have an idea," I said. "But everyone please tell me if it's really stupid *and* you have a better one: Walter, can you open the signet ring by rubbing it on the ground?—Don't do it yet—I'm just thinking—then, if you could use your fingers to fling the contents of the ring toward the fire—maybe, maybe one of the ingredients, like the phosphorous, will be flammable, and maybe there's an ember somewhere in the fire that will ignite it and keep us unfrozen for the night. And even if it doesn't, the sun tomorrow might ignite the fire in time to thaw us out."

No one had any better ideas and, after a short discussion, Walter prepared to implement this far-fetched strategy. I kept torturing myself to think if there were something better to do with our one dubious asset. I began to shiver badly, and was using my last inner resources, as I suspected the others were. With painstaking concentration and narrating as he went, Walter rubbed his right ring finger on the frozen sandy dirt of the desert. After trying several times, he managed to catch the signet ring's cover on a small, jutting stone and pried it open. Then, he closed it up again so that he would practice flinging the contents of the ring toward the stomped-out fire, about two feet away. Finally, he pried the ring open the second time. He waited for the wind to still. Then, as we all said a silent prayer, he snapped his wrist and sent the longevity minerals to the one place where they couldn't possibly cause anyone to live any longer.

CHAPTER 21

"You will have a bright future."

—Recent fortune cookie

WHAT DOES IT MEAN TO SAY that "time stood still"? Perhaps that we stand still, in fear and anticipation, while time moves forward? There was total silence from my companions as we awaited the results of our seemingly final bid for survival.

The desert noises seemed louder as we waited. I could hear night owls and coyotes in the distance. They might just be feasting on us soon if we didn't have a fire to deter them.

As we waited for any sign of combustion, I felt a touch on the tip of my right middle finger. Instinctively, I pulled back, thinking it was another nasty desert insect, or even our old scorpion friend, back for a return visit. But no. It was the longest finger of Ned's left hand reaching out to touch my hand. We had been placed so strategically that no other physical contact was possible. But as I moved my finger back to his, and turned my head to smile at him best I could, I felt his human warmth connect to me and offer comfort.

I swallowed hard and tried not to let tears run down my nearly frozen cheeks. We were so exposed there, lying on our backs with our faces to the night sky, facing eternity. Ned's small human point of contact called me back once more into our mortal world.

And as he did, a spark also flew up from the once dead fire! Against all odds, it was working! The wind must have carried some small bit of something highly combustible to ignite perhaps the one moribund ember still alive in the scattered campfire.

We aren't going to die! We aren't going to die! I exulted silently. I'll live to enjoy sunsets and French toast with maple syrup and... and... my mind flailed about, as the top of my head grew warmer and the warmth began to spread down my body towards my icy toes.

I smiled at Ned for real this time. I hadn't realized how resigned I'd been to the worst, while at the same time trying any practical means to avoid it.

Of course, we weren't really saved, but being pulled back this one step from frozen death was cause for exultation. Like most people pulled back from the brink, we took a moment to be thankful for our lives and to vow to live better ones before the usual petty discomforts, concerns and ambitions flooded over us again. After a while of relishing our reprieve, doubts began to set in again. We probably weren't going to freeze immediately. That was good. But hopes for getting out of Chaco Canyon seemed dimmer as time went on and the fire burned less brightly.

"I'd like to make a confession," Walter said suddenly, with a quaver in his voice. "Just in case no one finds us alive. I had always hoped to live to at least 100. That seems unlikely now. I have a need to say this, so you may as well know. As Schaeffer rightly perceived, I have been trying to slow down the search for Simon." He paused while the others, expressed disbelief and disgust. "Let me continue," Walter said sulkily. "We...I, well, Terry Franchot and I thought that it would be best for the research center if this scandal over the lost Oñate vessel played itself out over time, so that we, I mean, Terry, could persuade the Board of the research center to vote E.J. out as executive director. She's really not our sort of person, you know. And I did lower myself down the side of the cliff at Acoma Pueblo. Of course, I never thought I'd fall as far as I did."

This confession was met with silence. I was still feeling too relieved by the warmth of the fire to get angry again and pleased that my suspicions had at least been accurate.

Finally Ned said, "That was a really stupid thing to do, Walter. You jeopardized all our lives. You put the vessel in danger. What were you thinking?" He paused. "But, I have a confession, too," he said quietly. I gasped inaudibly. What would Ned say? What had he done? Would he jeopardize his future?

"When I was a young man," Ned said, "I did a very stupid and unethical thing. To get myself out of money trouble, I transferred an asset—that is, in plain terms, I sold an artifact to a private collector that should have remained in public hands. In Pueblo Indian hands, to be specific. I've felt wretched about it ever since. And I've wanted to make amends. I simply don't know how. I've lived with the uncertainty and fear all this time that someone would find out and humiliate me and never give me a decent job again in the field that I love. I hoped if I could find the Oñate vessel, then perhaps somehow it would set things right."

Silence again. Good. Now Veronica had no hold over him. He had freed himself.

And what did I have to confess? Many things. That I had coveted my neighbor's boyfriend; that is, Michael back at the detective agency, when I knew he was committed to another; that I had made a hash of my two marriages, leading to the murderous confrontation with Nick, my second husband; that I'd given in too often to self-pity, wound-licking and despair; and that, just today, I had let Simon out of my sight and possibly to his death at the hands of Gomez-Ibañes and Roberto. Why? Because I wasn't good enough at my job. But this was no one's business but mine, and I had no intention of sharing. Anyhow, I hoped to live and have another chance to make up for it. All of it.

Veronica spoke finally against the star-filled sky and the lonely animal sounds of Chaco Canyon. "Well, I might as well confess, too." Another pause. What new revelations were to come? "I'm only here because I wanted the Oñate vessel for myself. I would have kept it somewhere safe and let its whereabouts be known only to a few close friends. I didn't know how I was going to get it, but I wanted the chance."

"Oh," added Veronica, "I was the one who bought Ned's purloined artifact. But now I've sold it so it's off my hands. And sadly, now I can't hold it over his head any more."

Veronica didn't really sound sorry. Actually, she sounded peeved at herself for 1) not getting her way, and 2) telling hidden aspects of her past to underlings... and we were all underlings. But I noted that she—and Ned—kept one secret back—their affair. I expected such a gentlemanly restraint from Ned, and I also admired Veronica. Even in confession, the better-mannered generation understood the contemporary concept of "too much information."

We fell silent and relished the crackle and glow of the campfire still burning at medium force. Looking up, we could see the sparks rising into the night air.

I said quietly, quoting *Job*, "Man is born to sorrow as the sparks fly upward." Not an upbeat comment, I admit, but this might yet be my last chance for a literary allusion.

We lay there in silence, connected and apart, and thought our separate thoughts, hoped our separate hopes, and fought our separate fears. Suddenly, I was aware of movement from beyond the fire's circle of light. Yes, I'd heard it. Could it be a bobcat or coyote? It seemed to be the sound of someone or something breaking the icy ground as it came closer. Had Gomez-Ibañes and Roberto seen the light from the fire and come back to finish us off? Had I outwitted myself?

CHAPTER 22

"The magic of these pueblo dwellers has always been strong, older than the medicine of the Navajos and more potent."

—Tony Hillerman, The Blessing Way

I WASN'T PREPARED for the sight that I was to see, as the figure approached the campfire slowly and deliberately. I had seen Simon for only a few moments this morning—was it only this morning?—as he ran out of Earl's Restaurant, but I had gotten a good look at him. Tall, lithe, well-built, with long hair in a braid down his back and beautiful bronze skin with strong features. The Simon I saw standing in front of me was a beaten, broken relation to that man—but at least he was alive.

His head had been battered and blood was sticking to his hair. One eye was swollen shut, and across his chest, his shirt and skin below had been slashed through with a razor in an odd pattern of slashes, somewhat resembling the sign for "#" or a crude tic-tac-toe board.

He stood up in front of us, and then swaying forward as though he were going to faint, he dropped to his knees and squatted between me and Ned next to the fire.

"Simon?" I asked tentatively

"Yes," he said.

"Are you all right?"

He gave a bitter laugh in return. "Gomez-Ibañes and Roberto," he said, and pointed to his chest.

"Simon, if you can untie me," I said gently, "I can help you."

After a pause, Simon silently got to his feet. It looked as though this took a mighty effort. He walked back into his tent and came back with a knife. Then he cut the ropes on my feet and then my two hands.

I sat up slowly, instinctively rubbing my hands and, after asking silent permission, I took the knife from him and cut through Ned's ropes. Ned sat up and put his arms around me.

We held each other for a moment without saying anything. Somehow, there seemed to be sadness in this embrace, not relief, but maybe I couldn't read it right. Would I be seeing Ned again or was this the last time? Had his confession made it impossible for him to go back? Or was it something else? I pulled back and looked at him, losing myself for one moment in the depth of his beautiful sad eyes. Then, I remembered the knife, and our colleagues still tied up. I handed the knife to Ned and turned back to Simon.

"Simon," I said, "can we get you some water?"

He nodded quietly. I went back to his tent and found a bottle of water and handed it to him. Then I found a blanket to wrap him in, and our crackers and chocolate, and gave him some.

He wasn't bleeding now, but I wondered whether his cut ought to be cleaned. The others had gathered around the fine now, silently, sharing the snack food as though it were Beef Wellington and Pinot Noir.

"Simon," I said, sitting close to him near the fire, "Who did this to you? Are you badly hurt?"

Philip stared quietly into the fire, seeming to concentrate on getting warmer, fed and gathering his strength.

"Gomez-Ibañes," he said shortly. "He's mad, you know."

"I know," I said.

"He left me for dead. Carved me up like one of his crazy Penitentes and bashed me in the head. Thought I was dead."

"Those cuts on your chest, you said like the 'Penitentes.'"

"Gomez-Ibañes belongs to a Spanish cult—it was a Catholic sect, but they've all been excommunicated. They're on their own now. They act out Christ's agony with self-flagellation and, on Easter, they nail one of their own to a cross. Sometimes he dies. They make a mark like a double cross on each other to let the blood flow freely. This is their mark." He showed us.

"Should we clean off your head and chest? Do you have a first aid kit?"

"I don't know," he said quietly. Then he sighed, "Yes, I'll have to get moving again. It would be good to have a bandage."

I went back to the shelves in Simon's tent and got out a standard issue first aid kit. I took out gauze and peroxide for cleaning, and some large bandages. Carefully, I wet the gauze patches with peroxide and applied them to the swollen gouge on Philip's head; he was stoic throughout. Then I asked him to lift up his sweatshirt and I applied peroxide to the slashes.

These weren't deep, decorative only, and had closed up sufficiently not to need bandages. "Maybe you'll need a tetanus shot tomorrow," I said.

"Yes," he said. "Tomorrow," and he stood up slowly.

"Where are you going?" I asked worriedly. He looked much too wobbly to go anywhere.

"I'm going after Gomez-Ibañes," he said quietly. "He has the Oñate cup."

"But why do you want this cup so badly?"

"It's not the signature. It's the ancient Pueblo writing on it. The cup itself. It's the key."

"The key to what, Simon? Why do you need it?"

"The key to all my work," he replied and then turned away, effectively closing the conversation.

As he turned on his heels and went back to his tent to collect his belongings, I thought about my next move. If I stuck with Simon, I'd have my best chance to find Gomez-Ibañes and the vessel. But could Simon in his battered state and I take Gomez-Ibañes and Roberto? Maybe. Maybe with the element of surprise on our side. After all, Gomez-Ibañes expected us to be dead or about to be dead shortly, which, from his perspective, made it unlikely that we'd pop up at his place of business.

"Simon, do you know why we're here?"

"Gomez-Ibañes told me. He told me about Dorothea, too. He seemed to take pleasure in it."

I could see grief and anger rising in him, but he stifled a sob.

"Can I come with you?" I asked, "Maybe I can help you. And after we have the cup, and you've studied it, we can return it to the research center."

All I got in response was a shrug of shoulders. "I'll take that as a 'yes,'" I said and went back to tell the others that I was ditching them in the desert.

"Hey," I said, "it's getting light, but the ground is frozen. You'll get back to the Subaru with no trouble. And as soon as I get to a telephone, I'll make sure someone knows you're up here."

After some mild squawking, especially from Walter, I took my leave, squeezing Ned's hand for longer than necessary. I had a bad feeling about leaving him, but I didn't see much choice. As for Walter and Veronica, if I never saw them again it would be too soon.

CHAPTER 23

"There was once a man who had to take a long journey...."

—*The Brothers Grimm*, The Lady and the Lion

I TOLD SIMON THAT I'D DRIVE while he rested and we got into his old Jeep, which reminded me very much of my old black Jeep back in the driveway in front of my cozy yellow cottage in North Arlington, Virginia. How far away I'd come in this quest, driving through the frozen New Mexican desert with a Hopi archaeo-astronomer at my side, looking for a certifiable Spaniard from a sado-masochistic religious cult. When you put it that way, I wondered if I'd gone a tiny bit astray in choosing a profession.

As I drove out of the northeast side of Chaco Canyon on Simon's instructions, I stole glances at his handsome and determined profile. What makes an American Indian look Native American? And could someone who lived among them tell a Hopi from a Pueblo from the mutually hated Navajo or Apache? What I saw was a thoughtful man in his mid-thirties, well- tanned skin and a strong forehead, nose and chin. The eye that I could see, not the bruised one, was dark and focused in front of him. His cheek was lined, tear-stained, smudged with dirt. He had heard of the death of his wife that night and had very nearly met his own. Yet under the weariness, I could sense an unflagging will.

"Simon," I said gently, when we had covered about ten slow miles, "Why don't you get some rest? Just tell me where we're headed when we leave the Canyon and I promise to get you there."

After a while, he answered, "I think Gomez-Ibañes will have gone to his Morada in Abiquiu."

"Okay," I said. "What's a Morada and where's Abiquiu?"

After a long pause, Simon roused himself to answer. "A Morada is the building where the Penitentes worship, the cult that Gomez-Ibañes and his minions belong to. The Penitentes came from Spain with the Franciscan Brothers, who colonized us and stole our religion and way of life. But they went too far in emulating Christ's agony, with Lenten processions of self-flagellation and initiation rites where special members—Sangramientos, I think they're called—lashed the initiates until they passed out. Three lashes for the Trinity, seven lashes for the wounds of Christ, and so on. And then there are the memorial Crucifixions on Good Friday, where the volunteers—it is an honor—often died on the cross. They say that their bodies are buried upright in the earth and marked with mounds of stone.

"But why Gomez-Ibañes?"

"Oh, it's part of his 'proud' Spanish ancestry. The Penitentes today are all white males, descended from Spaniards. Juan de Oñate, the Conquistador of New Mexico, is their hero and saint. Some say he was a Penitente, and privately flagellated himself on his first Easter, when he and his soldiers stopped, south of El Paso, on his way north along El Camino Real to conquer the New Mexican Indians."

"Ah, Oñate," I echoed. "For Philip it's a religion indeed."

I drove slowly and carefully north on the dirt road still frozen from the icy night before. The Jeep rattled against the hardened tire ruts. The sun was rising magnificently in the east, all red, orange and violet. Alas, I was never really a fan of sunrises—not a proper hour for aesthetic appreciation. If you got up too early, you'd just be too tired to watch really good sunsets. As someone quipped after Benjamin Franklin: "Early to rise and early to bed, makes a man healthy and wealthy and dead."

In the hour of driving out of Chaco that followed, Simon told me more about the "Morada," derivation unknown, the Penitente's house of worship. Because Penitentes were outlawed and had to practice in secret, Moradas were usually built in out of the way places, without windows so that no one could look it. They usually had two rooms, a chapel-like room in front and a room for the Brothers' secret rituals in the back. Women were never allowed in. I gathered that if Gomez-Ibañes had taken the Oñate vessel to the Morada, it would never be seen again.

Philip Gomez-Ibañes's Morada was in Abiquiu, a town northeast of Chaco and Northwest of Santa Fe. Abiquiu, he said, was famous because the artist, Georgia O'Keefe, built her house there, and the sun-filled landscapes, red striated cliff sides, and desert with whitened animal skulls became familiar to people as what the Southwest looked like. I mostly recalled Georgia O'Keefe's paintings of flowers, but I seemed to recall a bony, chalk-like skull or two. Simon told me to turn right when we got to the northern edge of Chaco Canyon and to follow signs to Abiquiu. Then I felt him relax a little and, finally, his head nestled against the window and he slept. He had still not told me why he needed the Oñate vessel so badly or how he had come into possession of it.

As I drove, I worked out the only scenarios I could think of for how Simon had gotten possession of the vessel. His wife, Dorothea, could have smuggled it out of the locked vault for him. How else could he have taken it? Or perhaps Simon had taken the keys to the vault from Dorothea without her knowing it. That would explain the note of apology that he had left her in San Juan Pueblo. Either way, he had left Dorothea unharmed. Gomez-Ibañes and Roberto had come later and, not finding the keys or the vessel, had attacked Dorothea and left her there to die. Because she wouldn't say where it was or who had taken it? Because she had tried to protect Simon? I shuddered to think of Dorothea's last moments of consciousness. Had she refused to tell? Had Gomez-Ibañes threatened her and Roberto held her arms and covered her mouth so that she couldn't scream? I didn't want to think about it, and it was worse to think that Simon also had these pictures in his mind, narrated with pleasure by Gomez-Ibañes himself, while Roberto smirked in the background.

And now Simon and I were on our way again to find that cursed vessel. I couldn't think of any scenario in which someone wouldn't get hurt. I just didn't want it to be Simon and me.

I had driven to the northern edge of Chaco Canyon as Philip had instructed me, and headed northeast off the dirt road onto a paved two-lane highway. I drove for about 40 minutes toward the rising sun over the desert, a vista that's supposed to induce hopeful feelings, but which I only found ominous.

Finally, as my companion still slept, I saw signs for Abiquiu. I needed directions now, so I stopped for gas at a two-pump station and nudged him gently.

"Simon," I said, "We're here."

He struggled awake, no doubt wanting to forget everything and straining against the first terrible thought in his waking consciousness: that Dorothea was dead because of him. Regret, grief and anger must have mingled with the ache of day-old wounds.

I left Simon in the car as I pumped the gas and bought us each two cans of diet Coke and vanilla Tastee Cakes in a package. It was that kind of pit stop. No piping hot coffee or powdered red jelly doughnuts that could get a person going for a very hard day to come.

Simon was awake and alert when I got back to the car with my meager rations. He had moved into the driver's seat and I took the passenger's side. Without speaking, he turned the Jeep off to the left up a steep mountain road, which became dirt-topped and stony after a few hundred yards. There were no signs on this road, but he seemed to know where he was going.

The road wound higher and higher; it was desolate, abandoned country on either side. The sun had gone behind a cloud now and in the shadow of the mountain the sky looked low and threatening. At last we got to the crest of the road and started heading down on the other side. The road flattened out into a high plain, empty of signs of human life or habitation and covered with sparse outcroppings of scrub grass and small dry bushes. As we rounded the final bend, we were confronted with an ominous sight.

CHAPTER 24

"You don't get all your questions answered in this world."

—Gwendolyn Brooks, from Winnie

RELIGIOUS EDIFICES COME, of course, in all sizes and shapes. There are Buddhist temples and Quaker meeting houses, Ashrams, Mosques, Synagogues, and ornate faux-Gothic Catholic Churches, but there's usually a welcoming quality about them. There's a sense that a pilgrim, a wayfarer in this world of woe, an individual in need of sanctuary or a quiet and uplifting place, would be welcome to enter.

At the boundaries of the plot of land that housed the Penitentes' Morada, on the other hand, visitors were greeted with two denuded tree limbs stuck in the ground and supporting a thick rusted chain, which held a sign that read "No Trespassing" in large white letters on a black background. About 50 yards from the warning sign, past barren packed earth, was a bleak, dark-brown adobe structure, about two stories high, 60 feet long, and 30 feet wide, completely devoid of windows or other openings for natural light.

On closer look, there had been windows on one side of the building, but they had been boarded up with plywood slabs. On the roof of the structure, at the end where a church's altar would be, was an odd, rusted machine that looked like a cross between a wind-powered electric generator and an evil crone's spinning wheel in a Grimm's fairy tale. There was also a coarse wooden ladder leaning against the side without the windows, which reached several rungs above the roof.

Near the back of the building, three hand-hewn wooden crosses were visible, the center one having a terrifyingly primitive carving of Christ in great agony on the Cross, now weathered and faded. Hadn't Philip Gomez-Ibañes shown me such a similar artifact in his office at the Palace of the Governors? On a hill on the other side, another wooden figure of Christ, dressed in red, struggled up the incline carrying a wooden cross nearly four times his size. Barbed wire enclosed the whole site but it sagged in places, seemed not to have been patched in some time, and contributed to the derelict and foreboding impression.

With an involuntary shudder, I turned to Simon, who had stopped the Jeep some 30 feet from the barbed wire and was staring at the fortress-like Morada, his forearms resting wearily on the steering wheel.

"They must be asleep," he said, pointing to the familiar red low-rider parked on the far side from us, in the front of the building. "After a good day's work," he added with bitterness.

"What do you want to do?" I said, feeling apprehensive. First, our enemies were camping out in a protected fortress and we weren't. Second, the place was really creeping me out. But I had come this far, and my fledgling pride wouldn't let me back down now.

"I think that we should go separately. One of us goes to the front door and gets taken inside. One of us goes up the ladder and lets himself in through the roof. Element of surprise."

"Yes. The proverbial element of surprise. That always works. *Not.*" I said skeptically.

"All right," Simon answered. "What's your idea?"

"Well," I said, "we could go to the police station in Abiquiu and get some back-up?"

"Right," he said. "Let them slip away. And I'll never get the vessel. Besides, the police will never take Gomez-Ibañes—he knows the governor, the mayor, all the rich land owners—everyone in New Mexico. He'll blame it all on Roberto and everyone will believe him."

Simon posed a difficult ethical question for me: my job was only to get the Oñate vessel back, not to make all right in the universe. It wouldn't be my fault if Gomez-Ibañes was never punished for Dorothea's murder. Roberto deserved plenty of retributive justice anyway. And yet, we had a real chance to set things right. Putting aside my clear mortal danger and questionable vigilante justifications, I could really see Simon's argument. Men like Gomez-Ibañes don't really deserve to live to kill another day.

"Okay, Simon," I said finally. "I'm in. Do you want to be victim number one or victim number two?"

He let out a dry laugh. "You go to the front door and see if you can surprise them. I'll go in up the ladder and through the roof—there's usually a storage loft over the back room of these places, with a trap door through the ceiling to bring in provisions."

"I like the plan, Simon, but why don't you go in through the front door with your intimidating firearm, and I'll drop in through the roof if it becomes necessary."

Simon considered for a moment and agreed. He went through the instructions and the layout of the Morada a second time. Then he backed up his Jeep and hid it as best he could behind a rise in the dirt road. I don't know where he found the strength for all this, having lost his wife and all beaten and battered, but he checked his gun for ammunition and we got out of the car. We made our way as quietly and quickly as we could to our appointed places of entry, he towards the front door, where I lost sight of him, I to the ladder resting against the back adobe wall of what would have been the nave.

I can't tell you how quiet and forbidding the building and site were. The boarded up windows helped give us cover for our surprise attack, but they added a sinister element to the place. And while we had the element of surprise, I supposed that Gomez-Ibañes and Roberto had other compensatory resources within.

In a few seconds my hands grasped the rough ladder and I went up the widely-spaced rungs quickly. The ladder was rough-hewn but sturdy and I was on top of the roof way too soon. Peering over the top, I saw a small square outline of a trap door with a rope handle just as Simon had predicted. I opened it very carefully and could see in the gloom a short ladder leading down to a loft storage area covered with straw and stocked with bags of corn flour, huge cans of corn and beans, hanging peppers, and great vats of wine and oil—enough to withstand a month's long siege.

I moved quietly down the inside ladder and closed the trap door of the roof over me. I found myself in a crouch required by the low ceiling but I heard no noises below in what would be the back room for private rituals. It was dry and dusty in the attic storeroom and I hoped I wouldn't cough.

As I crept to the edge of this loft, I could get an angle on the room below: a dingy, stark, adobe room filled with a number of awful and hard-to-identify objects. This was indeed the back room where, as Simon had explained, the Penitente Brotherhood held initiations and performed sado-masochistic rituals, the better to know divinity by experiencing agony. Most disturbing, at the back of the room, was a black-draped altar decorated with skulls at the four corners. They looked real from where

I was squatting, grinning oddly as skulls seem to do. On the altar was also a black-painted wooden candelabrum, and on a side ledge were lanterns, some with candles, some with kerosene wicks. The lanterns were of pressed tin, with religious designs on their sides. A wooden figure of Christ in extreme agony, his ribs protruding and blood draining from his eyes and mouth, was nailed to a life-size cross, leaning against a wall. Yes, I remembered seeing a figure like that in Philip Gomez-Ibañes's office in the Palace of the Governors. Next to that figure, on a crude wooden shelf was a collection of home-made whips of braided rope or plant fiber, which looked to be some four feet long, and next to them a pot of water—to make them heavier and more painful?

And more. Next to the whips was a collection of sharp stones and jagged pieces of glass, which were used perhaps on Simon in his ritual scoring. A tub, filled with murky red water, completed the ghoulish picture. Was it for mercifully washing the penitents' wounds?

Finally, on the third wall was a sight even more grotesque: a carved skeleton carrying a hatchet was sitting in a cart filled with heavy stones. I didn't want to think about what this could mean or what one would do with them. I just wanted to get out of this house of death alive.

I was squatting out of sight in my loft, thinking these grim thoughts when voices entered my range. Simon was talking loudly and soon I saw him backing Philip Gomez-Ibañes into the back room, within my eyesight, using the barrel of his gun as an incentive.

"Get me the Oñate vessel now," Simon said loudly. "I'll kill you. I will. What you did to Dorothea." His voice was cracking badly and the gun in his hand looked unsteady.

Gomez-Ibañes was speaking loudly but nervously, stalling for time, hoping to attract back-up. "But I don't have the Oñate vessel here, Simon, now do I?"

"Get it for me, Gomez-Ibañes. Get it for me now," Simon repeated, his voice a little stronger.

Gomez-Ibañes had retreated against the far wall and had vanished from my view in the loft. I thought I could hear sounds as though he were opening a cabinet.

"Now, Philip. I need it now," I heard Simon say. He was obviously out of patience and on the edge.

Gomez-Ibañes walked slowly back into my view holding a wrapped parcel, which had probably been in the canvas bag when we saw him last. "Here it is, Simon," Gomez-Ibañes said tauntingly. "You'll never get it, you know, you half-blood scum," he added with indescribable hatred and scorn.

Simon let the safety off his gun now and moved closer to Philip Gomez-Ibañes. Suddenly, from behind Simon, Roberto came barreling out from the front chapel and grabbed Simon's arms. I screamed to warn Simon—too late—but at the same moment, I jumped off from the loft feet first and, using my best left Golden Rooster kick, I managed to connect my foot with Roberto's neck before I fell to the floor, bruised and winded.

But Roberto was down, Gomez-Ibañes was off balance and Simon had a chance to pick up his gun and hit the struggling Roberto with a skull-cracking blow on the back of the head.

Simon and I both turned to Gomez-Ibañes now, who looked shaken and ashen-colored.

"You bastards," he said. "I'll never let you or your kind have the Oñate vessel." And with that, he raised the parcel over his head and, with a cry of pain, smashed it on the stone floor.

CHAPTER 25

"I am an imbecile. I see only half of the picture."

—Hercule Poirot

W ELL, I DON'T NEED TO DWELL ON THE AFTERMATH of this sorry scene. There was stunned silence. There was Simon on his knees gathering every shattered shard of the broken vessel and packing it carefully away in a specimen bag. There was the tying up of Gomez-Ibañes' hands, who without the backup of Roberto, offered no resistance. I tied Roberto up, too, though he was completely unconscious, and then drove Simon, and Gomez-Ibañes to Abiquiu to find the Police Station.

From there I also called the park rangers in Chaco Canyon to make sure that Ned, Walter and the redoubtable Veronica had made it out of the park.

Finally, and reluctantly, I called E.J., who was extremely worried about all of us and more manically energetic than usual. I told her that we were basically all okay, some better than others, and that we'd be back at the center by late afternoon, as soon as we'd done the police paperwork.

Finally, I had to tell E.J. about the condition of the Oñate vessel. She had been too distraught to ask.

"Uh, E.J., about the vessel," I began.

"I don't care about that wretched vessel," E.J. broke in. "It wasn't worth Dorothea's life—obviously—and it isn't worth putting any other lives in danger. I'm sorry I ever cared. I'm sorry that I started any of this. I don't need to run a center. I can play golf at the Parental Country Club. I can wear lime green Bermuda shorts and brogues with tassels."

"E.J.," I interrupted. "The good news is that we found the vessel."

"And the bad news?" she said, understanding that this report was going nowhere but south.

"The bad news is that Gomez-Ibañes—when he couldn't have the vessel himself— purposely smashed it into a hundred pieces."

I heard a long sigh at the other end and then silence as E.J. was clearly sparing me her choicest litany of swear words.

"Hey, as I said," she continued finally, "who needs that piece of rotten, old Fiestaware anyway? Come on back, Schaeffer, and we'll have a stiff drink and commiserate."

ஜஜஜ

After crying and laughing with E.J. back at the center, and filling her in on all of the happenings, I called our Santa Fe police officer with the shiny hair, Lisa Gabriel. She, E.J. and I decided to call a meeting of all those concerned in E.J.'s office the next morning to see if we could tie up some loose ends.

When I arrived at E.J.'s office early the next morning, she was already there. She looked subdued and disheartened, perhaps for one of the few times in her life. I sat down next to her and looked about the same, though I'm probably more used to the feeling. Here we were at the end of the road. Dorothea was still dead, and the Oñate vessel—our Maltese Falcon, as it were—was smashed to smithereens. My case was a failure from any angle. I hadn't found the Oñate vessel in time to save it. My new boss back in McLean at the Will Thompson Detective Agency would berate me and probably let me go. Worst of all, I had let down my friend.

Probably E.J. would be fired by the Board, lose the new-found respect of her family, and the arrogant Terry Franchot would be made executive director or maybe King. Or maybe the center would close its doors, the staff all to be dismissed, and the scholars and artists to be exiled from this sublime place, sent home to their daily lives in Waco or Pittsburgh. The priceless Native American artifacts would be auctioned to private Japanese collectors and never be seen by the public again, and the center would be sold to the Marriott chain, which would put in a Starbucks where the beloved parakeet graveyard used to be.

But I digress.

Soon E.J. and I were joined by our fellow searchers and suspects. Dr. Walter Scoggins came in exuding his unique combination of impishness and sheepishness. Ned strode in quietly, sat down, and stared at his wing-tipped shoes. I couldn't catch his eye. Veronica made a regal entrance in full fawn suede jacket and another fabulously expensive pair of boots made from the skin of an exotic animal from a distant continent. She lowered herself down on the couch next to Ned proclaiming silently that now that she had arrived, the meeting could begin.

Next, Terry Franchot came in, looking well-fed and plumped up, his sleek hair like a satin pillow. His cock-of-the-walk bearing intimated that the royal crown would soon be his. His eyes scanned what would, he thought, soon be his office and, as we say in Washington, he mentally measured the drapes.

"Welcome, welcome," he said to Officer Gabriel as she entered the room and, unbelievably, he picked a yellow flower from the vase on E.J.'s desk and handed it to Officer Gabriel, who flushed and looked uncomfortable, not knowing where to put it. A uniformed officer had followed her in, accompanying Philip Gomez-Ibañes, and she handed it to the officer, who looked really puzzled.

Philip Gomez-Ibañes himself was rumpled and exhausted, but maintained his dignity, looking scornfully at me in particular, as though it were my fault that pride had led him to a life of covetousness, my fault that his sense of entitlement had led him to destroy the prized object that he had sought so hard and so ruthlessly to possess. Gomez-Ibañes was in custody but spared the indignity of handcuffs.

Finally, Simon Yahouti came in bruised, bandaged and beaten, seeming both angry and grief-stricken. Ned made room for him on the couch and Veronica begrudgingly moved over a millimeter.

Officer Gabriel took a pencil and notebook out of her carrier bag, sat up straighter and addressed the group.

"As you know," she began, "I have already taken statements from each of you, and we have partially solved the crime of the death of Dorothea Yahouti. Roberto Hernandez, an associate of Mr. Gomez-Ibañes and fellow member of the Order of Spanish etc., has confessed to assault and battery. He stated that he drove to the research center on Wednesday with Mr. Gomez-Ibañes with the purpose of borrowing the key to Vault One from Dorothea Yahouti. When Dorothea refused to open the vault for them and extract the Oñate vessel, Roberto says that he hit her with the handle of his gun, never meaning to kill her, but only to knock her unconscious while he used her key to the vault. Roberto has testified that he got the key out of Dorothea's pocket, opened the vault, and..." she paused for effect, "found that there was an empty space on the special pedestal on which the Oñate vessel was supposed to be. In rage and frustration, Roberto said, he took out his knife and slit one of Ms. Yahouti's ankles, as a reminder of the vengeance that Oñate's men took on the Acoma Pueblo Indians. Roberto seemed to think that Dorothea's husband Simon, who is part Acoma Pueblo himself, had gotten to the vessel before him, and he took his anger out on Dorothea.

"Mr. Philip Gomez-Ibañes, for his part, claims to have been waiting outside in Roberto's vehicle all this time and says that he had no knowledge of this attack—only that the Oñate vessel was not in Vault One when Roberto looked for it there."

Philip Gomez-Ibañes stared at each one of us in turn, daring us to disagree. Simon stared back with hatred and contempt.

"Since there are no impartial witnesses to this crime," Officer Gabriel continued, "at least no witnesses who have yet come forward, it will be a matter for a jury to decide on the guilt or innocence of each party." She paused and, turning the page of her notebook, she began anew.

"We are here today to try to piece together what happened to the Oñate vessel before Mr. Gomez-Ibañes obtained possession of it yesterday, and destroyed it by smashing it on the ground in full view of Mr. Simon Yahouti and Ms. Schaeffer Cornell. Mr. Yahouti collected the numerous broken shards at the scene and has handed them to me for safekeeping.

"Let us now begin with you, Ms. Lowell, as the director of the research center."

E.J. had just taken a big gulp of orange juice, which she endeavored to swallow. With a bit of her characteristic spunk, she began:

"A week or so ago, Dorothea came to me and told me that she suspected someone had tampered with the pedestal holding the Oñate vessel. She thought she had noticed that the glass casing had been replaced in a slightly altered way, though she couldn't be sure. She said that she noticed this while she was giving a docent tour, and she was sure that she had not let anyone inside the red velvet rope surrounding the pedestal. She said that she had already mentioned her suspicions to Ned. Later that day, Ned came to discuss this with me and we determined to be on guard and wait to see if another incident occurred.

"We waited and watched to see if anything else happened. I didn't want to call in the police—because nothing was missing—and I didn't want to cause unnecessary concern or attention from the center's Board. Finally, I decided on a middle course. Several days ago—it seems so much longer—I called my old college friend Schaeffer here. She isn't an artist or the great niece of Joseph Cornell—"

(There were audible gasps while everyone turned to look at me with disapproval.)

"Obviously not," Veronica pronounced loudly. "Her feeling for art is inexpressibly poor."

"But," continued E.J., " Schaeffer Brown is a licensed private investigator, and I knew that I could trust her." E.J. smiled at me.

"Why did you choose to associate yourself as a close blood relation to a distinguished artist like Joseph Cornell, anyway?" Veronica asked me. "There are so many less talented artists you could have chosen."

"I like him," I said. "And I like the idea of containers holding odd, juxtaposed things, secrets, clues, answers…"

"As though a container could ever do that," Ned added mournfully.

I decided to pick up the narrative at that point.

"Well, in any case, the day that E.J. picked me up and brought me back to the center, Dorothea had just been attacked and the Oñate vessel was gone."

"I might add," said Officer Gabriel, artfully fluffing her ponytail in Terry Franchot's direction, "that we dusted for prints that night and found only those we'd expect to see: yours, E.J., Ned's, Dorothea's, Terry's, and those of other fellows at the center. Anyone else who had touched the pedestal had to be wearing gloves."

"Readily available at the front desk," Terry said, smiling at Officer Gabriel. "We require them for scholars handling any artifacts. And a good thing, too. If I had my way on security issues, none of this would have happened," he concluded, with an odd mixture of triumph and appropriate solemnity.

"Thank you, Terry." E.J. said wearily. "We will certainly look into security measures in the future."

Terry sat up straight in his chair, preening as if he had just made a surprising and wise observation and everyone had applauded. Was I the only one there who wanted to take his well-fed face and slap him repeatedly on alternate cheeks with a satisfying whap, whap, whap sound?

But I continued seriously, "E.J., Ned and I went the next morning to the San Juan Pueblo to notify Dorothea's relatives in person, and to see whether we could locate Simon Yahouti, Dorothea's husband. He was not at San Juan Pueblo but had left a note for Dorothea, saying that he was sorry for what he was about to do. We assumed that he meant that he had stolen the Oñate vessel without Dorothea's approval, and we thought we should find him as soon as possible. The Governor of San Juan Pueblo, a cousin of Dorothea's, suggested we look for Simon at Acoma Pueblo, in his mother's house there, or in Gallup, where he had a part-time job, or in Chaco Canyon, where he pursued his archeological research.

"The next morning, Ned, Veronica, Walter, and I set off to find Simon. We followed him to Acoma Pueblo and to Gallup. We finally found him in Chaco Canyon last night—or rather he found us and saved our lives after we were all left tied to stakes in the ground by Philip Gomez-Ibañes and Roberto, and left to die of cold or predator attacks. When Simon, nearly dead himself, finally came and found us, he told us that he had had the Oñate vessel but that Gomez-Ibañes and Roberto had taken the vessel from him and administered a savage beating, leaving him to die as well.

"We should probably now ask Simon to fill in his part of the story because we know that the vessel was in his hands until Mr. Gomez-Ibañes took it forcefully away from him in Chaco Canyon."

Simon sighed, sank lower on the couch, and spoke emphatically, but with the pain of loss as well as his injuries. "First," he said, "I never touched the Oñate vessel or its blasted pedestal until the time I took it away. So if there was any monkeying with it before that, or changing the position of the glass that Dorothea reported, I had nothing to do with that. Someone else will have to answer for that.

"And it wasn't Dorothea either. She loved me, but she would not help me take the vessel. She was loyal to you, E.J., and to you, Ned, and she was honored by the work you gave her and the trust you put in her."

He sunk into silence.

"I stole the vessel," he said finally. "I took it when Dorothea was giving a tour of the Navajo weavings in Vault Two. I had taken the key from her earlier and made another copy. I needed that vessel. It was standing between me and the work I have been doing over the last 12 years.

"As some of you know, I was trained in archaeology at the University of New Mexico, and I immersed myself in the area of archeology that demonstrates that our Pueblo ancestors were great astronomers, that the axis of their magnificent dwelling places like Mesa Verde in Colorado, Chaco Canyon here and even at Paquimé in Chihuahua, Mexico, are all related to each other geographically and spiritually. They are all on the same parallel, and all were positioned to follow the sun, moon and stars in a yearly cycle.

"Many people do not believe this. They find my research fanciful—"

Gomez-Ibañes stood up and interrupted "A useless, baseless attempt to show the worth of these primitive civilizations!"

And just as quickly, Simon jumped up and was at his throat. "Murderer," he said under his breath, his faced flushed with the effort of trying to choke Gomez-Ibañes.

Officer Gabriel and the armed policeman guarding Gomez-Ibañes were on Simon right away and subdued him, seating him back on the couch. This time the armed policeman kept his position next to Simon instead of Gomez-Ibañes. The policeman's right hand flexed as though he were preparing to use his firearm if necessary.

Simon was still trembling with anger as he continued his story. "I needed the vessel. Not to keep, not to have, but to take with me to Chaco Canyon and test a major hypothesis in my work. As you know, in addition to the signature on the bottom of the vessel, which might or might not have been inscribed by Oñate in the 17th century, the ancient Pueblo symbols on the sides are far older, probably from before the Millennium, and are very unusual. They match very nearly some of the petroglyphs that I discovered in an unexcavated area northeast of Casa Bonita in Chaco Canyon. The petrographs are of the sun, a man perhaps pointing, a constellation, and what looks like an exploding star. Not only do the pictures themselves and their relationship to each other match closely to those in the Canyon, but there is a space, a niche, I found in the architecture of the kiva wall, which the vessel would fit exactly—I believed—and make a repeating pattern of three pointing to a far away object in the night sky. I needed the vessel to see if the exact grooves of the bowl fit into the place I had found for it. I needed to have that bowl for one night, at the spring equinox on March 22nd this year, to see how the moon and stars looked from that vantage point, to see what my ancestors had seen on a similar night 1000 years ago." Philip paused. "Or maybe even 2000 years ago. The unexcavated kiva that I found was much older in origin than the others. Could the exploding star that my ancestors saw have been from the time of Christ?

"So I stole the vessel and didn't look back. I drove to Acoma Pueblo to my mother's old house there, where I keep my detailed notations. The goons showed up shortly afterwards, I understand. Then I drove on to Gallup where I keep my digging materials, my tent, and my old Jeep, and from there I drove into Chaco Canyon, the goons always at my back, I suspect. I didn't look back. I just had to know.

"It was getting to be dusk when I entered the canyon from the southwest; I stopped briefly at the visitor's center and picked up some water. I drove to the exact location that my years of research had taken me to. I set up my tent and got out my telescope and my equipment for measurement. I don't know how Gomez-Ibañes and his crony tracked me there, but they found me, they took the Oñate vessel from me, they beat me, slashed my chest with their ritualistic blood symbols, and left me there, unconscious, in the desert to die." Simon paused and continued slowly, "But not before I got to place the vessel in its place at the very ancient kiva I had discovered."

There was a collective gasp and a sense of anticipation as Simon paused to collect his thoughts.

"I found the exact spot that I had identified. I checked my notebooks, got out my telescope and my angle-measuring devices, calibrated as I had planned to the changes of the Earth's movement over time. With a fine paintbrush, I dusted off what seemed the outline of an indentation to hold the vessel built into the rock wall, and I removed the Oñate vessel from its protective pouch and carefully placed it in.

"It very nearly fit—but not quite. To my astonishment, the contours of the cup did not quite line up. I couldn't believe it. I tried it in slightly different positions. Had all my study and calculations been wrong? It was hard to comprehend."

"At that point, the goon squad showed up, took the vessel, and attacked me. And that's the end of my story—except for one last thing."

"Schaeffer and I decided to go after Gomez-Ibañes. I had a very good idea of where he would go, where he thought he would hide his stolen prize far from prying eyes until the uproar died down. Maybe you don't know that our kindly center board member is also a member of an outlawed religious order, the Penitentes, who practice in secret in closed and hidden Moradas, and indulge in sado-masochistic practices—flagellation, realistic reenactments of the Crucifixion, and ritual cutting." Here Simon stopped, and unbuttoning his shirt, exposed his freshly scarred chest."

There was another collective gasp.

"So Schaeffer drove me to the Morada north of Abiquiu and we saw Gomez-Ibañes and Roberto's car there. We managed to surprise them, but in the end, Gomez-Ibañes smashed the vessel on the stone floor of the inner chamber and it splintered, as you've heard, into a hundred pieces." Here Simon paused again and collected himself.

"With the fighting over, I got down on the stone floor and picked up every single piece of the vessel and placed the shards carefully in one of my plastic specimen pouches. Schaeffer drove me to San Juan Pueblo and left me off there for the night. After I'd slept a little, I opened the pouch and was able to study the pieces calmly in daylight. What I found out astonished me. It was clear. The Oñate vessel was a fraud! It wasn't old at all. It was cast recently! It was a total hoax. And for this hoax, Dorothea died."

"Are you sure, Simon?" E.J. asked.

"Completely sure. I gave Officer Gabriel the pieces this morning. Send them to a lab and see whether these fragments are more than 1000 years old or even 400 years old."

Officer Gabriel nodded to the armed policeman and he pulled a plastic bag of broken pottery out of his satchel, walked over, handed it to E.J. and remained there standing by us. I recognized the bag of shards that Simon had so laboriously collected in Abiquiu.

"That does raise a question or two," I speculated slowly. "Was the Oñate vessel a fake from the beginning? Or did someone substitute a fake one and now has possession of the real one?"

"Aha," Terry said at once. "More skullduggery. This place is worse than a—I don't know—than an English department. It has all the professionalism of a bowling league. It—"

"All right, Terry," E.J. cut in. "Point taken. Yes, the research center is run on trust for everyone's professionalism and good will, and if that's a bad thing, I don't know what a good thing would be," she finished somewhat lamely.

I turned to Ned and asked him how he had authenticated the pot when he first found it in the "attic" of the center.

Ned sounded puzzled but sure of what happened. "Well, when I first spotted the Oñate vessel among a number of miscellaneous objects, I knew that we had a significant find. I am an expert on many archaeological periods of this geographical area, and I could tell right away that this was a very old pot, that the markings were unusual, and that the signature on the bottom might or might not be authentic. If it were authentic, the pot would indeed have rare value. So of course, I showed it to E.J. and Terry, and to Dorothea. And then I asked Veronica to come and take a look at it. She has an excellent eye. And then she brought in Gomez-Ibañes, who is an expert on Don Juan de Oñate, and then we asked Simon to come see it to certify to its age, and several other members of the board of directors. We all agreed that we had something remarkable.

"And then of course we sent it off to the lab at the University of Arizona, which verified the date as circa A.D. 1000 and the authenticity of the Anasazi markings. They were not as definitive about the Oñate signature."

"So if Simon is correct now," I concluded, "and I have no doubt that he is, we are dealing with two pots: a fake one in shards in a plastic baggie and the real one somewhere else, and, I hope, in better condition."

I surveyed the assorted guests around the room, each looking at the others with suspicion. Several people had been prepared to kill or to die to get their hands on the fake vessel—Simon and Gomez-Ibañes in particular—which suggested to me that they were probably unaware that they were pursuing a replica. This observation saddened me. I would have so liked to pin another crime on Gomez-Ibañes's shopping list.

That left, among others, Veronica and Ned, Walter and Terry. Any of them could have stolen it, had a replica made, and sold it on the black market—they all had the connections—or they could have stolen it and kept it hidden in their private collections, even though they knew that it couldn't be publicly acknowledged. Ned had admitted his weakness to me, and his past association with Veronica. I had seen them in close, private conference in the car at Acoma Pueblo—what could that have meant?— and Veronica had a fanatical need to collect, to own rare and beautiful objects. Could I believe Ned when he told me he had atoned for his past? Was Veronica's "deathbed" confession tied to a stake in the Chaco Canyon desert authentic?

Then there was Terry. He was certainly trying to create trouble for E.J. and show that she was incapable of running the research center. Walter Scoggins had admitted as much—that he was actively slowing down our search in order to help his pal Terry. I was going to discount Walter Scoggins as too feckless and also too focused on his longevity studies. I could see him as the accomplice, but never the crook... the London gangster lackey, but not Professor Moriarty. Still, was his deep silliness a front?

To be thorough, in my own mind, I had to count E.J. as a suspect. I couldn't quite glean her motive unless it was money. Was the research center in financial trouble and in need of a big illicit sale—which the Board would never approve—in order to continue its existence? This unfortunate line of thought led to another. Did she call on me as an expert P.I. because she really doubted my abilities and surmised that I would never find the trail of the vessel or finger the real culprit? There was a great movie with that plot—yes! *Body Heat*, in which Kathleen Turner hired William Hurt, the worst detective she could find, in order to substantiate her alibi.

But no. This was E.J. I was speculating so negatively about. I knew that she did not have it in her nature to be underhanded or disloyal. She could flop on her face and often did, but it would be a grand flop, and above-board.

As I was thus speculating, as Officer Gabriel was no doubt wondering if she had missed anything during her previous search of the premises, and as the others sat lost in thought, two things happened so quickly that I wasn't quite sure how they came about.

It started when Gomez-Ibañes got up quietly and crossed the room to where E.J. and I were sitting, seemingly to examine the contents of the plastic pouch filled with the shards of the replica vessel that E.J. was holding. But instead, he took a last quick step to the uniformed officer next to us, grabbed the gun from its holster and spun around, pointing it wildly towards the others. The stunned police officer moved quickly to stop him from firing the gun and, at the same time, in one movement, I sprang up and tried to pull Gomez-Ibañes's arms down as well. The three of us wrestled with the gun for what seemed like an endless moment and then, shockingly, instead of stopping Gomez-Ibañes, one of us managed to fire the gun off by mistake. The loud discharge sent us all backward, and at the same time we heard the splintering of pottery: a bullet had pierced one of the painted ceramic statues of E.J.'s aunts' beloved parakeets—maybe Maria Callas—and it was hit squarely.

Then Terry Franchot fainted.

CHAPTER 26

"Don't count your chickens. When it's time to eat, you'll know.

—*Gwendlyn Katz-Spielberg*

Fʀᴏᴍ ᴛʜᴀᴛ ᴍᴏᴍᴇɴᴛ ᴏɴ, things began to unwind to their natural conclusion. The newly re-armed police officer took Gomez-Ibañes away, in handcuffs this time, and Officer Gabriel tried to revive Terry Franchot by splashing cold water on his face. Unfortunately, mouth-to-mouth resuscitation had not proved necessary.

Slowly then I understood. There was only one person in the room who demonstrated an extreme reaction to the incident. The gunshot was startling, of course, but no one else blacked out. Terry's fainting had to involve something that only he knew about that had almost happened to one of the parakeet ceramics—and it probably had nothing to do with his fondness for birds. He must have known that something of value had been hidden in one of them.

There were eleven ceramic birds left untouched. I nodded to E.J. and she nodded back at me, and one by one I lifted each intact parakeet commemorative and shook it gently. When I came to Robespierre, number eight, we heard the movement of a soft object within. I held Robespierre out to E.J. and she carefully lifted the object out, removed the extensive wrapping, and showed us all the real Oñate vessel, intact and able to make trouble another day.

It turned out, as we had surmised, that Terry had wanted to subvert E.J.'s authority by demonstrating her unfitness for the position to the research center's Board and taking her place after she was fired. What I hadn't guessed is that Terry was so aggressively manipulative that he had undertaken such a bold scheme to get to the top. It was clear now that Terry had taken the original vessel—that must have been the tampering on the pedestal that Dorothea had noticed—made a replica, and placed the real vessel in a safe place where people were unlikely to look. At some point, after E.J. was gone, Terry must have planned to "find" it somehow, and be a hero.

Is hiding a pot in a ceramic parakeet technically a crime?

Certainly the consequences were grave. Simon's exultation at finding the vessel was muted by his terrible loss. It made me think more about the pride in ancestry and wonder why I was so sympathetic to Simon's kind and so antipathetic to Gomez-Ibañes's. Was one really better than the other? Did it redound in any way on a living person that his ancestors had done either wonderful or terrible things? Simon would have to wait a full year until the stars were aligned again to try the vessel in Chaco Canyon. It was better that way, I think.

Our little gathering was getting to be the kind of nightmare party where everyone wants to leave but is too tired to go home. E.J. finally roused herself and said to the assembled cast, "Well! Problem solved. You can all go now. Terry, I'll expect your resignation letter by close of business today. I'll write a report to the Board about this sad matter, and I'll announce the time and place for a memorial service for Dorothea Yahouti shortly. Any questions?"

Walter Scoggins raised his hand. "I have some new research material that I'd like to share with the fellows. Are we having sherry here in your office as usual before dinner tonight?"

"I'm glad you mentioned that, Walter. Yes, *we* will be having sherry as usual tonight. *You* will be having sherry elsewhere. For your part in abetting Terry's underhanded schemes, you are hereby barred from the research center in Santa Fe in perpetuity. I'll include your part of the story in my note to the Board."

"But, but—" he sputtered, "If it weren't for Terry and me, the Oñate vessel would have been destroyed."

"Nevertheless," said E.J. and folded her arms.

ꊠꊠꊠ

Later, E.J. and I got some chips, salsa, and coffee from the center kitchen and sat in her office together.

"I can't believe it's over." E.J. said. "I knew you could do it—I'm so glad I called you. Thank you, Schaeffer. If there's anything I can do for you, ever—"

"I'm so glad for you, E.J. This is a wonderful place. And you're a great executive director. It's just important to weed out the nasty and the dangerous."

"I think we've pretty much done that. Will Gomez-Ibañes go to jail, do you think?"

"I don't know. I hope his lawyer gets him to plead out. I don't want to have to testify at the trial. I never want to see Gomez-Ibañes or Roberto again."

"And what about ever seeing Ned again?" E.J. asked with a sly smile. "I'm not blind, you know."

 barbarbar

As it happens I saw Ned again later that morning, right outside of the bird cemetery near my room. We sat together on a wrought-iron bench nearby in the sun.

"Thank you," Ned said. "For saving my livelihood, my good name."

I quoted Iago back to him, " 'He who steals my purse steals trash; but he who steals my reputation…' "

He laughed. "We always used to chuckle in class about why Iago carried a purse. But I mean it, Schaeffer. I can't tell you what it means to me to have the vessel back and Terry gone. E.J. and I can do great things for the center and for the Native communities we serve. If there's ever anything I can do for you—"

"Thanks, Ned. I'll keep that in mind."

He paused.

"I should tell you, too, that you helped get Veronica and me back together again."

"I did?"

"I know that she's an arrogant pill, but we go way back. We understand each other—passions, weaknesses and all."

"Oh." Was all I could muster.

"I adore you, Schaeffer. You're wonderful. I loved our adventure together. It brought me to life again. But we don't live in the same world."

Perhaps you think I inhabit the third moon of the planet Twyla? I thought to myself.

"Mmm." I said.

He took me by the shoulders and kissed my forehead—a very bad sign.

Then he walked back to the center's main building. There was still a mournfulness, a resignedness about him as he walked away, even though this was probably the happiest day of his adult life. What was it that made me attracted to these qualities?

ﾛﾛﾛ

Dorothea Yahouti's memorial was held the next day in San Juan Pueblo, in the community's sacred space, its kiwa. The Mayor of the Pueblo and her next of kin presided. Simon, E.J., Ned, Dorothea's fellow docents and I attended with about 30 friends and neighbors from the Pueblo. Simon spoke movingly about how Dorothea had enriched his life and how he would try to live up to her memory. E.J. said a few words about her beauty, knowledge and integrity. A small group of young dancers did a sacred dance, and the Mayor concluded the ceremony in the Tewa language. As I recalled from our visit to Acoma, the Pueblos were not afraid of death like the Navajos, but they did not welcome it either.

I was on my way home via the Albuquerque airport shuttle. The landscape I had thought of as barren just a few days ago was now beautiful and familiar to me. I had re-kindled a friendship with E.J. and had learned many new ways that people can fail to live together in peace. I had the makings of a great new ethnic wardrobe, and only a few bad bruises on various parts of my body, no major injuries like last time. I had tasted my first genuine huevos rancheros, stared down my first scorpion and had helped fire a shot from a loaded gun.

The plane ride back to Virginia was uneventful and I returned to the office the next day. Heidi, the underage receptionist, was at her station applying lip gloss with a cherry aroma when I got there. She buzzed Rich to let him know I was back.

Rich was strangely welcoming to me, suspiciously so. He gave me a big smile and warm greeting. Then, he explained to me that he had just received a Fed Ex'd letter from E.J. touting my great detective work and, more to the point, a gigantic check from her which, he claimed, "would certainly help the net net bottom line."

"Too bad it's after Christmas," he added, "Or you'd be in for a big bonus."

Heidi told me that Michael and Marna were both out on assignment. I wasn't ready to face Michael yet in any case. I couldn't risk a second also-ran in the space of one week, so I decided to take the day off. I called my best friend, Rachel, and we agreed to dine out that night on Tex-Mex and tales of the American Southwest.

Rachel and I were just settling in at the Austin Grill, munching on tortilla chips and raising our first margaritas in a toast to adventure, when my cell phone rang. It's impossible for me to ignore a ringing phone—even if I'm in a shower or I'm morally certain that it's someone I don't know who wants to sell me car insurance. So I took a quick sip of margarita and slipped open my iPhone.

Surprisingly, it was Rich, my awful boss. The margarita turned to day-old ice-cube water in my mouth.

"So, Schaeffer," he began. "I have a new case for you."

"You do?" I managed to say.

"Yes, indeed," Rich said. "Can you be in Shanghai by the end of the week?"

"Absolutely," I gulped.

"I'll fill you in tomorrow. This could lead to windfall profits. Bye."

"Rachel, you'll never believe this," I said with a tentative smile. "I may be going to China."

"That's exciting!" she replied. She saw my dubious look and added, "We just finished toasting the life of adventure."

"But I'll have to learn some Chinese—all I can say now is 'General Tso's Chicken'—and I don't know the customs, or the manners, or the geography and everyone over there does T'ai Chi better than I do. I can barely function as a P.I. on my own turf!"

Adventure, yes, I thought. But wasn't Confucius quoted in his *Anelects* saying, "He who learns but does not think, is lost! He who thinks but does not learn is in great danger." So many ways to go wrong. The Master's saying had my name written all over it.

I ordered a pot of strong green tea.

ACKNOWLEDGMENTS

I want to thank my daughter, Wendy, for her life-saving suggestions on plot twists, her creation of a whole line of chicken folk wisdom and for introducing us to a certain Daniel Spielberg. I want to thank my son, Jonathan, for his clever and beautiful cover art on both Schaeffer books, and for bringing wonderful Ashley into our family. Special thanks to Harry for being Harry.

Thank you as well to Warren Conner, an inspired teacher of T'ai Chi (taichicenter.com). Warren teaches the real thing and is in no way responsible for the depiction of T'ai Chi in these pages.

Naturally, all of the characters in this story are made up. This is fiction. To my knowledge, no one has yet found the Oñate vessel.

CANDACE KATZ is deputy director of the President's Committee on the Arts and the Humanities. She holds a Ph.D. in English from Harvard University, a J.D. from Georgetown University, and is a registered private investigator in the Commonwealth of Virginia.

Breinigsville, PA USA
08 October 2010
246956BV00007B/2/P